I0730278

A DARK ROMANCE NOVELLA

Limerence

BEC EDEN

Copyright © 2025 by Bec Eden

All rights reserved.

No part of this publication may be reproduced, stored, or transmitted in any form or by any means, electronic, mechanical, photocopying, recording, scanning, or otherwise without written permission from the publisher. It is illegal to copy this book, post it to a website, or distribute it by any other means without permission.

This novel is entirely a work of fiction. The names, characters, and incidents portrayed in it are the work of the authors imagination. Any resemblance to actual persons living or dead, events, or localities is entirely coincidental.

No generative artificial intelligence (AI) was used in the writing of this book. The author expressly prohibits any entity from using this publication for purposes of training AI technologies to generate text, including, but not limited to, technologies that are capable of generating works in the same style or genre as this publication.

Bec Eden asserts the moral rights to be identified as the author of this work.

Cover design by Line Book Cover Design

Chapter design by MGS Desiigns

Editing by Danyelle Briggs

Proofreading by Erin Page of Erin Writes Romance

ISBN (eBook): 978-1-7637582-2-3

ISBN (paperback): 978-1-7637582-3-0

Content Warnings

This story is written for those over the age of eighteen. It contains scenes and topics that may be distressing. These include: stalking, attempted rape (not by MMC), a taboo relationship involving a therapist and client, inappropriate professional behavior of a therapist, murder, and discussion of domestic abuse.

Additionally, there are frequent, detailed sex scenes that involve primal play, edging, restraint, exhibitionism, and voyeurism.

If you are uncomfortable or unsure about any of these topics then I recommend protecting your mental health by not reading this book. Alternatively, you can always reach out to me directly for more information.

To my family: if you've picked up this book, please don't read chapters one, two, three ... actually just don't even read this one. Seriously. Please don't.

For Kelsey,
Whose terrible dating stories inspired the pug mug.

Limerence

Limerence

Noun

The state of being obsessively infatuated with someone, usually accompanied by delusions of or a desire for an intense romantic relationship with that person.

Nate

> @huntern8 aren't you getting bored with your current obsession? You've been doing the same thing for over a month. All you do is follow her and take photos for your spank bank. Time to step it up, my man.

I lounge on my sofa, the only light in the room coming from my phone screen, and re-read his message for the tenth time. I ponder Apexpredator69's question and wonder if he's right. *Am I getting bored?* Maybe a little. But, god, do I love those photos I've taken. My totally normal, not at all concerning check-ins on Hunted—the digital playground for people like me who "gather intel" on unsuspecting strangers—usually make me wonder if I've been playing it too safe. I love her. I need her. And these grainy little snapshots? They're starting to piss me off.

I didn't realize how much I needed Hunted until I found it. A place full of people who get it—who get me. Here, I can talk about my obsession without judgment. Here, people understand that obsession and love go hand in hand. Hell, I might even be one of the more stable ones. That's ... probably not a good thing.

I think about ways to spice things up, to make the chase more thrilling. I know her schedule. I follow her whenever I'm not stuck at work. But I want more. I *need* more. I want to speak to her. Touch her. Watch her bleed if only a little bit. Just to see how far I can push her. I wouldn't really hurt her—not much. I'm not a monster. But when I picture her slick with blood, my cock twitches. And yeah, maybe I'm more into the idea than I realized.

Maybe Apexpredator69 is right. Maybe it is time that I get closer.

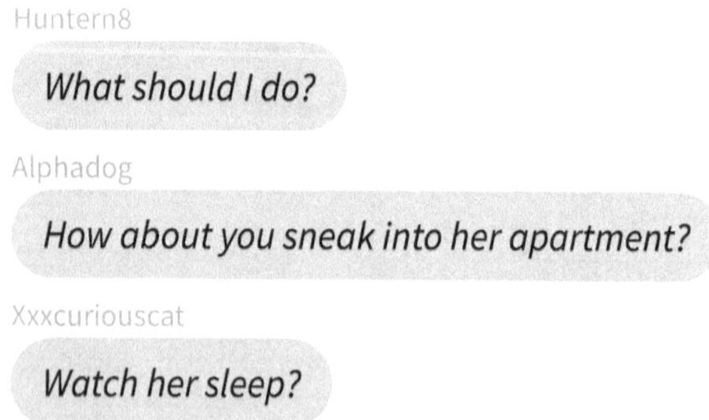

Could I actually do it? What if she caught me and called the cops? How would I talk my way out of that? The fear is there but it fades fast, buried under the comfort of the fantasy. I imagine her asleep. Probably wearing tiny sleep shorts and a flimsy top. Or better—nothing at all. I see myself slipping into her bedroom, the moonlight casting shadows across her skin, her blonde hair fanned across the pillow like a halo. In my daydreams, I trace a finger over her soft, parted lips. Then lower, cupping her full breasts, and they're everything I imagined and more. She doesn't move. Doesn't stir. Just lies there, chest rising and falling.

I bet she's even more beautiful in sleep.

The notification sound from my phone pulls me out of my imagination, and I'm not surprised to find that my hand has ventured down my pants to wrap around myself in a punishing grip. One of these days, I will have her.

Apexpredator69

> *What does she do for work? Can you see her there?*

Yes. Yes, I can. It's something I've already been thinking of, but I've been apprehensive about taking that step. When I watch her from afar, I can convince myself that she loves me too, that we are made for each other. What if that illusion shatters when we actually meet? What if she doesn't like me? What if I scare her?

Huntern8

> *What if she doesn't like me?*

Apexpredator69

> *But what if she does?*

My body trembles with desire as I consider the possibility.

I close out of the site and lock my screen, plunging myself into darkness. It's well past midnight and I know I should sleep, but I'm far too wired for that. Just the idea of seeing Olivia more, talking to her, and touching her is enough to send me out of my mind with need.

I move into my bedroom for one purpose alone. I use the key behind the TV to unlock the small drawer in my nightstand. I sigh in relief as I take in the familiar sight of my collection of printed photos. Every single one of them is of *her*. There's nothing inherently sexual about the pictures. Most of them were taken discreetly while she was in public, but they're special to me regardless. I grasp the thick pile and spread it over my bed, before kneeling in the center with the love of my life surrounding me.

I gaze at her bright blue eyes, framed with large, thick glasses that draw even more attention to their beauty. Her blonde hair varies in style from picture to picture. I've learned that she prefers to wear it down at work. The long strands cascade around her shoulders in a silken sheet. That pin-straight skirt and tight blouse never fail to have me thickening in my pants. At the end of every day, she pulls her hair up in a messy bun, and, although she always looks beautiful, I have to say, I prefer her hair down. I'm desperate to run my hands through it, to grab a fistful and pull.

I let out a loud moan as I imagine the whimper that would escape her lips when I control her movements with my grip on her hair. She would pretend to want to escape, but we would both know that she loves it, that she wants more. I unzip my pants and take my weeping cock in my hand. The tip is already leaking precum, and I know—as usual—that it's going to take no time at all to find the release I need.

I begin to stroke myself firmly, just the way I like it. But instead of my hand, I picture her perfect, pouty lips wrapping around me. She would take me so well; I know it. My fantasy changes to what she would taste like, her lips, and her delicious cunt. I stare intently at one of my photos—the one with her lips slightly parted. I can almost hear what the breathy moans would sound like as I lick and suck at every inch of her.

I thrust into my hand more viciously, the familiar tightening of my balls signaling that I'm close as I keep the image in my mind. I pant out her name like my own personal prayer, and let out a hoarse cry as I shatter. Jets of cum spurt from my tip as I coat the photo closest to me. I watch in satisfaction as the substance coats her face and body. I reach down and use a finger to smear the cum over the photo so that no inch of visible skin is free from it.

One day, she will be covered in me for real.

She will look so perfect wearing my cum.

I hastily clean myself up and place the photos back into their hiding place, except for the one I ruined. I chuckle seeing it, knowing I can print a new copy. Before I settle into bed, I take another look at the business card that lies on top of my nightstand.

Olivia Kane

Licensed therapist

Ph: (504)234-7689

8138 Oak Street

New Orleans, LA

I drift to sleep with a smile, certain of one thing—tomorrow I'll be getting closer to my little devil.

Olivia

I rest my elbows on the desk and push my glasses back up from where they had slipped down my nose. I usually wear contacts at work, so the constant feeling of adjusting the glasses today annoys me. I let out a sigh and try to ground myself by doing some progressive muscle relaxation. I start at my toes, scrunching them up for five seconds before letting them relax. I work through my other muscle groups using the same process and feel the tension leaving my body.

My last client was challenging, and I have very little time to prepare for the next one, who will be here any minute. The man I will be seeing next is someone I haven't met before; he gave very little information when he made the appointment. I have no idea what to expect, which makes me a little apprehensive. Some of my clients are dangerous, so it's usually important for me to assess their risk before agreeing to see them.

I didn't this time—now I'm cursing my lapse in judgment.

A knock on my office door forces me to close my laptop and push back from the desk. My receptionist, Sophia, tells me that my client has arrived and completed the necessary paperwork. She hands me the papers, and I quickly scan his answers to the screening questions, praying that the lack of initial questioning isn't going to cost me

Name: Nate Holloway

Age: 32 years old

Occupation: Data analyst

Presenting problem: Obsessive Thoughts

Obsessive thoughts. That could mean anything—or everything. Still, it's a start. And right now, anything is better than going in blind. I smooth down my pencil skirt, run my fingers through my hair, and head to the waiting room to meet whoever this Nate Holloway is.

"Hi, Nate. I'm Olivia. It's nice to meet you," I say, offering a small smile as I gesture toward my office. "Come on in."

The man lifts his gaze to mine and I'm caught—trapped in the depths of his chocolate brown eyes, framed by lashes so long it's almost unfair for a man to have them. His warm brown hair, streaked with natural golden highlights, is just long enough to fall across his brow but not quite long enough to tie back. A neatly trimmed beard frames his sharp jawline, and I swear to god, this is the most attractive man I've ever seen. My heart pounds, heat curling low in my stomach as sharp, uninvited images of him and me—naked, tangled, gasping—rush through my mind unbidden and all too vivid. He clears his throat, jolting me back to reality. Mortification crashes over me as I realize that he's been standing, waiting for me to lead him to my office.

Oh my god. How long have I been standing here, blatantly ogling a stranger? A *client*?

Get a grip, Olivia.

Now.

"Oh, um … this way," I stammer, turning sharply and walking ahead, doing everything I can to hide the heat rising in my cheeks.

Once inside, I settle onto my usual spot on the sofa and gesture for him to take a seat on the one opposite me, doing my best to shake off the lingering embarrassment.

"So, what brings you here today?" I ask, forcing myself to push aside my earlier thoughts and focus on professionalism.

He shifts forward, settling on the sofa's edge, his body leaning toward me as if drawn in by some invisible force. His gaze locks onto mine, and I have to remind myself—*breathe, Olivia.*

"I'm having trouble getting someone off my mind," he replies. His voice is deep and rich, like the first sip of whiskey—smooth, warm, and entirely too intoxicating. The sound of it alone sends a shiver down my spine, heat creeping up my neck as I fight the ridiculous urge to blush. Of course, a man this attractive would have a voice to match.

"She's on my mind every second of every day. It's like my life revolves around her, and I can't do anything else."

I shift slightly, trying to ignore how his voice alone sends an unwelcome thrill through me. *Professionalism, Olivia.*

"Okay," I probe. "Who is this person to you, and what makes this such a problem for you?"

His gaze darkens, something unreadable flickering across his expression. "She's a stranger to me. We've never been properly introduced. But I know her better than probably anyone else. I know what she looks like when she's tired, stressed, or upset. The way she does her hair when she's trying to be professional, and the way she does it when she's trying to relax. I *know* her."

He pauses, his next words sending a chill down my spine.

"But she doesn't know me."

Oh.

Oh.

Those kinds of obsessive thoughts.

"So, you know all of this about her, but you've never actually met her?" He nods slowly, making my stomach tighten for reasons I don't want to examine. "What's stopping you?"

His lips part slightly before he answers, his voice dipping lower. "I love her. More than anything. But I like to ... watch her."

A shiver runs through me, and I can't tell if it's from unease or the way he so casually mentioned stalking a woman. "Does she know you do this?" I ask, trying to keep my voice steady despite the sudden dryness in my throat. He bites his lip and shakes his head.

Fuck. Why is that so attractive?

I take a breath, forcing myself to reset. "Let's take a step back for a moment. Can you tell me a bit about your history—your childhood, your family?"

For fifteen minutes, he talks about growing up with a single mother and no siblings. It sounds lonely, but he had, and still has, an amazing relationship with his mom.

And yet, I'm barely listening.

My gaze keeps drifting to his lips, wondering how they would feel on my skin, how they'd move against mine. Every time I catch myself slipping, I pull my focus back, nodding in all the right places, letting out small murmurs of acknowledgment—'mhmm's and 'tell me more about that's—but my mind is a traitor, lost in places it has no business wandering.

Does he notice? *God, I hope not.*

Eventually, I manage to pull myself together enough to steer the conversation back to what actually matters—his obsession. "What made you decide to seek therapy for this?" I ask, and for the first time in this session, he takes a moment to think before answering.

"I guess I wanted to talk to someone about her," he finally says. "I want someone to know how much I love her." There's a quiet sort of conviction in his voice, something that makes my stomach twist.

"Do you want the obsessive thoughts to go away?" I press, still trying to piece together what exactly he's hoping to get out of therapy. Because so far, I don't get the impression that he *wants* things to change. And that's usually a huge red flag for me.

"No!" he blurts out. I flinch at the sudden volume change. His eyes widen slightly.

"Sorry," he says, softer this time. "I mean, I don't *want* things to really change. I just need to get things off my chest—to talk about her, share my thoughts with someone else."

I nod. I've worked with people who form unhealthy attachments before, but *this* ... this is something else. He hasn't said it outright, but I'm pretty sure Nate is in *deep* stalker territory. The signs are all there, lining up too neatly for me to ignore. Carefully, I ask my next question. "Do you ever think about harming this woman?"

His reaction is immediate: "No, no, no. Never." Then, a pause. "Wait, that's a little bit of a lie. I would like to cause her pain," he admits. "But only consensually."

Another image flashes through my mind—Nate bending me over, spanking my ass until it's raw.

Fuck. What is this man doing to me?

An unsettling sensation coils low in my belly, and the realization hits—am I *jealous* of his obsession? The thought of being *hunted, stalked*, sends a thrill through me, one I shouldn't be feeling. That's all kinds of fucked up, right? Wanting to be stalked isn't exactly *normal*—and I would know. Not to mention the fact that fantasizing about a *client* is wildly inappropriate.

I clear my throat, forcing myself back to the present. "Can you tell me more about how you currently interact with her?"

His lips curve slightly. "I just follow her when I can, try to show up at places she frequents. Oh, and I take photos."

Okay. That's not great.

"Do you understand that this behavior would be considered stalking?"

He nods again. "I know, but I don't want to stop." A wistful smile plays on his lips.

I glance at the clock. Our time is up. I exhale slowly, steadying myself. "That's all for today. Thank you for coming in."

Would it be wrong to ask him to come back?

As if reading my mind, he asks, "Can I see you again next week?"

You can see me anytime you like.

"If you think it would be helpful, then sure. Just make another appointment with Sophia on your way out. We need to talk more about how this obsession is serving you right now, and why it may have developed."

As I lead him to the waiting room, his hand brushes my lower back—a light touch, warm, firm. A spark shoots straight through me. I should say something, *stop* this before it starts. But I don't. I let him keep it there until we reach the door.

"Thank you, Olivia," he murmurs in a deep, sultry voice. "It was so nice to meet you, and I can't wait to see you again next week."

Damn. Why does his voice make my panties wet?

"Bye," I manage with an awkward wave. Before I can turn, he catches my wrist, pulling me in just enough to press a slow, deliberate kiss to my cheek.

I freeze.

He pulls away, leaving me standing there, rooted in place, unable to move from the shock flooding me from where his lips just were.

I think I'm attracted to my client.

My hot as *fuck*, completely off limits, likely unhinged *client*.

Fuck me.

Olivia

That night, I can't stop thinking about what it would be like to have someone so obsessed with me that they follow my every move. *Honestly? It sounds exhilarating.* The rational part of my brain knows I should be freaked out. *Normal* people don't get excited about having a stalker. But I've always been … *adventurous* in my sexual encounters, and this is a new interest I never considered.

All week, I'm distracted, counting down the days until Nate's next appointment. I try to push him out of my mind. I use every psychology trick in the book to try and distract myself, but we all know it's much easier to give people advice than it is to take it.

Finally, Tuesday arrives, and I'm jittery on my way to the office. *This*—the nervous, electric anticipation—is *not* how I should feel about a client. I manage to get through my morning appointments well enough, nodding and responding as usual, and I doubt anyone would be able to tell that I didn't give a damn about what anyone was saying, *Fuck, I'm a bad therapist.*

Perched on the edge of my desk chair, I swipe on another layer of lipstick, pretending I'm not listening for Nate's arrival. But the moment I hear his deep voice greeting Sophia, I shoot to my feet, practically rushing into the waiting room to meet him. As I shut the office door behind us, Nate's gaze sweeps over me, appreciation flickering in his eyes. My spine straightens, heat creeping up my skin.

To be fair, I *did* dress up today.

Okay, maybe "dress up" isn't the right term, but I made sure I looked sexy *while still being professional.* My tight button-up blouse clings just right, one extra button undone to reveal the hint of my black lace bra. I've got great tits, and I wanted to show them off today. I also spent more time on my hair than usual. Loose waves frame my face, a small detail but one that always makes me feel sexier.

And judging by the fraction of a second too long that Nate stares at my chest, it was worth it. *I've got him.*

Maybe I can push this other girl out of his head.

No. That is not what I'm going to do. Don't go there, girl.

I start our session, trying my best to do what I'm supposed to do and help my client. The problem is that today, he seems less interested in discussing his obsession and more focused on getting to know me. Before I know it, we're flirting—chatting as if we're on a date, my professionalism dissolving by the second. I lean in too often, feigning interest in what he says, when really, I'm inviting him to look down my shirt. And from the way his pants are straining, he's *definitely* affected by me.

When I notice we're nearing the end of the session, I force myself to bring the discussion back to Nate. "Have you thought much about what we spoke about last week?" I ask. "The stalking behavior? Whether treating the obsessive thoughts might be helpful?"

He smiles, and my stomach flutters. "I've decided that I'm going to do a bit more with her," he says casually. "Actually meet her and show her how much I care."

I wince, but I try to smother it instantly. *That doesn't bother me. Not at all.*

"Oh, interesting. What are you planning on doing?"

"Just an introduction, for now. I don't want her to know about my ... obsessions right away."

Hmm.

"Do you think she would be afraid to find out that you've been doing this?" I ask.

"Would you be?"

I consider him, and somehow manage to stop what I think from escaping me. Truthfully, no. I don't think I would be afraid. Should I be? Absolutely. But there's just something about the idea that awakens some dormant part of me.

Instead of telling him all this, I deflect. "This isn't about me."

A slight frown touches his features before he leans forward, lips quirking. "Do you think I should start seeing you twice a week instead of weekly?"

I pretend to think about it for a moment before answering.

"Well, I suppose if you think that would be helpful …"

His dazzling smile makes my stomach flip. I want to run my fingers through his hair, trail them down his chest, down to—

Stop.

As he stands to leave, his hand finds my lower back again, lingering just a second too long. But this time, it slips lower, cupping my ass.

I *should* pull away.

But I don't.

My body reacts instantly, a shiver running down my spine, my blood heating at the pressure of his touch.

I am so fucked.

The next day, a package is delivered to me at work. Sophia is practically bursting with excitement when I finish a session and find it waiting for me.

"Oh my god! Who's sending you flowers and gifts?" she squeals.

An enormous bouquet of blue orchids—my favorite flower—rests beside a small, ribbon-wrapped box. My grin spreads before I can stop it. *Who could've sent these?*

"Is there a note or card that came with them? I ask Sophia.

She shakes her head. "No, they were delivered addressed to you with no other information," she responded.

A flicker of unease passes through me. "That's kind of weird, right?"

She shrugs her shoulders. "Maybe. I'd just be happy that someone bought me something," she laughs, and honestly, she's got a point. It's not every day that someone goes out of their way to do something nice for me. No one ever does anything like this for me.

I reach to pick up the small box and hastily unwrap the bow. "You've got to be kidding me!" I exclaim.

"What? What is it?" Sophia asks, darting around from behind her desk to see what I'm holding. "It's nothing creepy, is it?" All I can do is shake my head as I look down at the gorgeous coffee mug in my hands, covered in the most adorable pictures of pugs.

"Aww, that's so cute! What's the problem?"

It's not really a problem per se. Not only did I receive my favorite flowers, but now a mug with my favorite dog breed? There's no way this is a coincidence. I tell Sophia as much, and she doesn't seem at all perturbed.

"Guess you've got a secret admirer, you lucky thing," she tells me. My heart jolts at the thought. *A secret admirer?*

Any lingering unease fades as my thoughts drift to *who* might have made this grand gesture. I realize I have no idea—but maybe, if I'm lucky, they'll reach out again.

And, god help me ..., *the idea thrills me.*

Nate

"Olivia," I groan, thrusting into my fist, my movements frantic and driven by pure need.

This is getting out of hand. I thought I was obsessed before, but now that I've met her? *Fuck.* I'll never get enough. She is complete and utter perfection, and I need her like I need the air in my lungs.

I won't *really* be alive until I feel her tight, warm cunt squeezing around me, until I see my handprints on her ass and thighs, feel her nails raking down my back. I can already hear her moaning my name, begging for more, desperate for me to grip her tighter, fuck her harder.

"Fuck!" I bellow as I spill all over myself again.

My cock is going to need a fucking break.

The mere thought of Olivia gets me so hard that I can't think straight until I relieve the pressure. The number of times I've jacked off since our first session is unhealthy. Maybe I should tell her next time. Not that *she's* the reason for my obsession. Just that it's stronger than I expected.

Can you get carpal tunnel from jerking off?

I try to regain focus as I shower and wash off the evidence of my release, knowing full well that I'll be back in this same position another time or two today. I'm lucky that my job is incredibly flexible, and as long as I answer my phone in a timely manner and meet my deadlines, I can get away with a lot. I wonder what my boss would say if he knew this is how I am spending my work time.

I've been watching Olivia closer than ever, deep diving into her online presence. She's careful—nothing personal, nothing overly revealing. But I've found small details. Pieces of her that make her *her*.

They're *mine*.

It's been a few days since I had her favorite flowers and the pug mug delivered. I hope she loved them. *I know she did.* I did my research, after all. Olivia Kane grew up with a pet pug named Doug, and she's wanted one of her own ever since. But her apartment doesn't allow pets.

So, instead, she collects pug-related things. I've seen the occasional photo on her social media of a pug plush toy or a small pug statue. She's not obsessive with her interests, but I feel confident enough that this would make her happy.

If I'm ever going to convince her that I'm the man for her, I need as many wins as I can get. Not that I think it'll take much. She's already interested.

She wouldn't lean forward like that for *just* any client. She wouldn't wear that sexy black bra, biting that perfect lip, staring at me like I am her next meal. There's no way she would look at anyone else like that.

Only me.

There will only ever be me.

Over the next few days, my routine stays the same.

I wait outside her apartment in the morning, watching as she leaves, making sure she gets to work. Then, I do the same in the evening. It's not *stalking*—it's *protecting*. Not that I need to worry. In the months I've been watching her, she's only met up with people a handful of times. Just girls' nights.

She doesn't *really* like going out.

She prefers to be at home, binge-watching TV or reading. I wish I knew *what* she watches and *what* she reads, but she keeps that locked away from me. *For now.*

Today's Sunday: Farmers Market day. She really does make it easy for me to follow her every move. Her routine rarely changes.

I bring my camera to the market to stock up on photos for my collection. It's easy to capture pictures of her under the guise of photographing the market. She looks stunning today—she *always* does—but there's something about casual Sundays and watching her long blonde hair in a messy bun, her loose dress swaying with every step. I snap a photo at the exact moment the sunlight catches her face.

Perfection.

Now that we've met properly, I have to be far more careful about where I lurk. I don't want her to see me. If we run into each other once then that's okay—purely a coincidence—but she's more likely to recognize me in public now, and I don't want her to get suspicious.

A man greets her and she stops to talk to him. I growl under my breath when I realize I don't recognize him. Who *is* he? And why the *fuck* is he touching her arm like that? She laughs at something he says, and I see red.

No.

She *can't* laugh at another man. She *can't* look at someone else with those bright, wide eyes.

She's *mine.*

I don't even have time to think before I race towards them, with no plan other than to separate them. When I get close, I slow down and walk towards them, trying to look interested in something off to my right. I get close enough to Olivia that it's easy to accidentally bump into her when I walk past, causing her to launch forward. My bag of produce spills onto the ground.

"Oh shit, I'm so sorry," I say, pretending to be embarrassed. "I wasn't looking where I was going. Are you okay?"

I notice when she recognizes me, and familiarity lights up her eyes. "Nate! Hi, are you okay? Let me help you."

The other man—*Mr. No-Name*—lingers for a second before muttering, "I'll see you later, Liv."

Liv?

I suppress a growl as he walks away, barely an afterthought in her mind. *Mission accomplished.* Olivia crouches to pick up my things, and when our hands brush, a zap of electricity shoots through me. I hold her gaze, letting the moment linger.

She's *so* close. I could reach out, tuck that loose strand of hair behind her ear, tilt her chin up. She straightens before I can act on the thought.

"God, I'm so clumsy," I say with a sheepish smile. "I really am sorry."

She shakes her head. "It's fine. No harm done. I'll see you at our next session." She smiles. *Blushes.*

I smirk. "Can't wait."

As she turns to finish her shopping, I stay rooted in place, watching, making sure she doesn't stop for any other men.

Because if she does, I *can't* be held responsible for what happens next.

Nate

I stride into Olivia's office with more excitement than a golden retriever, flashing a charming smile at Sophia, the receptionist.

She looks up from her computer, eyebrows lifting. "Oh, hi there, Nate. You're a little early. Your appointment's not for another thirty minutes."

"Yeah, I know I'm early, but I was in the area already and just thought I'd hang out here."

That's the *official* reason.

The truth? I know that Olivia sees a client before me, and I need to see how they interact when she walks him out. I need to make sure that what I think is between us is there. I was also losing my mind with anticipation. I couldn't pace outside her office much longer without drawing attention, so here I am, *exactly* where I belong.

I kill time scrolling on my phone, but I'm not paying any attention. My ears strain for any sound, any laugh, any shift in her tone.

But I hear *nothing*.

Her office must be soundproofed.

Frustration burns through me, but the realization sparks something in me. How much noise does it *really* block out? Would little Sophia out here be able to hear Olivia scream, gasping my name, begging as I bend her over her desk and bury myself inside her?

Shit, now I'm hard again. I adjust myself discreetly, willing my pulse to slow. Time drags, but finally—*finally*—the door to her office opens.

I try not to look like I'm fucking her with my eyes, even though I am absolutely doing just that. A man walks out first—*young*, younger than me. The monster inside me bares its teeth.

Stay the fuck away from what's mine.

I scan Olivia instinctively, cataloging everything. No flesh exposed. No suggestive smiles. No lingering glances.

Good girl.

Then her gaze lands on *me*. Her bright blue eyes light up. A slow, beautiful smile spreads across her lips, and for a second, the air is knocked clean out of my lungs and warms my very soul.

She is *utter fucking perfection*.

Olivia

*D*own, girl.

Stop thinking about your client naked. Stop thinking about all the filthy things you'd let him do to you behind the closed door of your office.

Stop thinking. Stop thinking. *Fuck.*

But the harder I try, the worse it gets. I'm drenched just imagining myself on my knees, his cock stretching my lips, his fingers tangled in my hair as he fucks my mouth.

I squeeze my thighs together, pulse hammering. It's only been a few days since I saw him last, but I've been *desperate* for our next session.

Who's the one with obsessive thoughts now?

Somewhere, beneath the haze of lust turning me into a barely recognizable, wanton creature, I know I should *end* this. I need to terminate the therapeutic relationship before I destroy my entire career. I'm a *professional.* Until now, nothing has ever challenged that. I worked my ass off in college, built a reputation in this field, and yet ...

Tell that to my pussy.

She doesn't give a shit.

I say goodbye to the client I've just seen and tear my eyes away from the beautiful man waiting for me. I hold up a finger, letting him know I'll just be a minute. I make the conscious decision to tell the little angel Olivia that sits on my shoulder to fuck off for the day, because I'm going to follow the little slutty devil instead.

I turn back into my office, shutting the door behind me, pressing my back against it as I try to calm myself.

I'm going to do something incredibly stupid.

The idea of him seeing me like this—knowing what I'm doing—is too intoxicating to ignore.

Before I can second-guess myself, I untuck my white satin blouse from my pants and reach behind my back, unhooking my bra. The straps slide down my shoulders, and I slip them off completely, shoving the bra into my desk drawer. The cool silk of my blouse rubs against my bare skin, my already hardened nipples pressing against the thin fabric.

I specifically chose this one because it's slightly see-through.

Not obvious. Just enough. Enough to tease. Enough to push boundaries.

There's no denying he's attracted to me. I'm being careful, just in case I've read him wrong. I can have plausible deniability, but that care is about to go out the window.

I run a hand through my hair, shaking it out so it looks tousled, just fucked. Then, I walk to the door, open it, and smile. "Nate," I say sweetly. "Come in."

His eyes are drawn to my chest like laser beams are directing him, and I can see the exact moment he notices my lack of a bra. "Fuck," he exhales, running a hand through his hair. "Are you trying to kill me?"

"Whatever do you mean?" I ask, tilting my head.

His jaw tightens, his hand drifting toward his lap, adjusting himself. The motion is so blatant, so *unapologetic*, that heat licks up my spine.

He just groans, dropping into his seat. I should get this back on track. Keep things professional. But the professional went out the door the minute he walked in. Instead, I lean forward slightly, letting my blouse shift.

"So," I begin. "I want to talk a bit more today about the woman, the one you believe to be your true love."

His gaze stays locked on me, so *hungry* I feel it like a touch. "What do you want to know?"

"How did you find her?"

A wistful look softens his features. My hands clench in my lap. "The first time I saw her, she was in a coffee shop," he murmurs. "I was mesmerized. I knew right then that we were destined to be together."

My fists tighten further. My nails press into my palms.

"From there, I got a lot of my ideas on how to find and follow her from *Hunted*."

I frown. "What's that?"

He chuckles, shaking his head like he's letting me in on a secret. "Well ... it's a chat room for people who like to hunt—or to be hunted."

I blink. "A chat room for stalkers."

"And people who like to be stalked," he adds, his lips curving into a smile.

"That's ... a thing?"

"Yeah, it's quite common. Some people like to be explicitly hunted in a sexual way—it's called primal play. And then there are some who get off on the idea that someone is watching them."

I shift slightly in my seat. "So ... what do people post there?"

"Requests," he says easily. "Things like *wanted: someone to chase me through the woods at night and fuck me in the dirt.*"

A shiver rolls down my spine.

I should be disturbed. I should feel repulsed.

But instead, I feel ... *curious.*

Interested.

Turned on.

"So, what do you do there?"

He watches me like he's waiting for something. "Mostly just get advice. Talk to people who understand me and don't think I'm a creep for how I behave. I'm not interested in anyone else, so I don't bother to look through the posts."

My throat is dry. His eyes are locked on mine, pupils blown, voice deep and husky when he asks, "What do you think?"

I swallow. "About what?"

"Would you like it?" He murmurs. "Being watched. Chased. Hunted. Knowing you're always on someone's mind? That they can't stop thinking about you, can't stop watching you?"

My breathing is coming in short, desperate pants. I'm more turned on now than I have ever been in my life, and the glint in his eye tells me he is all too aware of it.

The room feels too small. My skin feels too hot. His attention is like a brand, burning into me, *owning* me.

The worst part? I don't hate it. I *want* it.

I follow his gaze to the clock, and we both notice that time is up. I let out the smallest moan, knowing that he's going to be leaving me here. Empty and wanting.

Nate smirks. He stands, moving toward me slowly. My breath stutters as he places his hands on the chair—one on each armrest, boxing me in. His forehead nearly touches mine, his breath warm against my lips.

He moves slowly, giving me time to move if needed, but I don't. I can't. I'm rooted here and nothing could move me from this spot. Then, suddenly, he shifts, burying his face in the crook of my neck with a low groan.

My whole body feels like it's been charged with electricity.

His scent surrounds me, something dark and musky, and I swear I feel *every inch* of him pressed against me. "You are everything," he whispers. Adoringly. Reverently.

His tongue drags along my neck, slow and deliberate, before his teeth graze my jaw. I barely hold back a whimper. Then, when I think I can't take any more, his fingers ghost over my nipple, rolling it between his thumb and forefinger. A sharp, teasing pinch. A flick.

My gasp is *loud*. My body is *on fire*.

And then—

He pulls away. "You taste even better than I imagined," he murmurs. "See you soon, little devil." The door clicks shut behind him. And I sit there, wrecked, panting, legs shaking, wondering what the *fuck* just happened.

Olivia

I have no idea how I made it through the rest of the workday after *that* session with Nate—if I can even call it a session. There was certainly no therapy happening in that office.

Somehow, I managed to put my bra back on and fake my way through the last few clients of the day. I don't think I remember anything that was discussed. I was too focused on my soaking wet panties and the raw need coursing through my body.

When my last session ended, I bolted from the office with a half-wave to Sophia, desperate to get home to look up *Hunted*.

The second my laptop boots up, I start searching. It takes longer than I expected—link after link, like it doesn't *want* to be found—but finally, I land on the page.

Hunted.

Without putting too much thought into it, I create a profile using the name Nate called me when he left today: *His.little.devil.*

I pause at the profile picture option. If this were ever to get out, my career would be over. Eventually, I settle on a random image from the internet. I'm only here to look after all.

My heart pounds as I scroll through the request section of the site. There are two parts: one for the hunters and the prey, and another for the Hunters, where they compare notes.

The more I read, the more my pulse thrums. I had no idea something like this existed. And now that I do, I won't be able to forget it. An exhilarating hunger—one I haven't felt in years—coils inside me. I haven't dated in a long time. The men I've been with? Boring. The sex? Adequate at best. I get off—well, *most* of the time. But there's always been something missing.

Now, I think I know what it is.

The chase. The hunt.

I *need* danger. I *need* darkness.

Maybe this is how I get it.

As I scroll, a particular username catches my eye.

Huntern8

Fuck, guys, I think she might be into me. I've been doing what you suggested—meeting her at her workplace, pretending to be a client. I'm sure she's coming on to me.

I read the username again.

Hunter-n-eight.

Hunter Nate.

Could this be ... *him*?

I click his profile, scanning his activity. He's in a private Hunters chat. I *need* to see that chat.

Without hesitation, I create a new account, this time selecting *Hunter* as my role. My request to join the private chat is pending, and I wait, restless, nerves buzzing. For a brief moment, it occurs to me that I might be the one acting unhinged now.

But that's a problem for another day. Right now, I'm investigating my client, hoping to learn more about his mystery woman. What will I do with that information? I have no fucking clue. I know I won't be able to sleep until I find out.

A notification pops up. Request approved. Messages flood the screen, hundreds of them. I scan for his name, my breath catching when I find a response to his latest post.

Alphadog

> *No way! That's awesome. You going to ask her out?*

Huntern8

> *Maybe… I think I want to fuck her in her office first. It's soundproofed and everything, and she has that sexy therapist look going on *wink emoji**

The air leaves my lungs, and my vision blurs as my brain pieces it all together.

Oh my god.

Nate's mystery woman.

It's *me*. I'm the one he's been following. The one he's been obsessing over. The one he's pretending to be a client for.

I should be horrified. Disgusted. Terrified.

But instead—

I *burn.*

My body feels like it's on fire as I consider what this might mean.

Do I confront him?

Or ...

Do I play along?

I close my laptop and try to extinguish the fire that consuming me. I'm not successful. Not even a little. So, I surrender to it.

I'm still wearing my shirt, but swapped my skirt for sweatpants. I glance at my living room window. The curtains are closed. My apartment is on the first floor, and although the window doesn't look out onto the street, I'm always conscious that people might be able to see straight into my apartment if I were to leave them open. Funnily enough, right now, that's exactly what I want. But not just anyone. *Him.*

Is he outside?

Some of his posts on Hunted seemed to indicate that he hangs around my apartment, just in case. I peek out into the darkness. I don't see anything, but that doesn't mean he's not there.

If he is watching, I'm going to give him a show.

The kind of release I need right now is not going to be achieved by just my fingers, so I grab my favorite toy from my bedroom before I position myself back on the sofa.

I strip off my sweatpants, leaving only a thin lace thong. I pause. Then, I discard *that* too.

In for a penny, in for a pound.

I spread my thighs on the couch, trailing my fingers down, teasing.

Am I really doing this?

But there's no stopping now.

The possibility of him watching—seeing me like this—has me soaked.

I reach a hand down, my finger applying light pressure to my clit. I close my eyes and let out a groan as the need for release increases, before moving further down. Fuck, I knew I was wet, but I'm absolutely dripping. I breach my entrance with one finger and then a second. I pump my fingers a few times, and my breathing quickens. As I suspected, it's not enough. I'm not full enough. I press the button on my bright pink rabbit vibrator, and a low hum fills the room. I move the large toy into position and slowly slide it inside myself, making sure to place the external part securely against my clit.

Yes, oh, fuck yes.

The second it slides inside me, my whole body shakes. My free hand tugs at my nipple, rolling it between my fingers. My head falls back, a moan ripping from my throat. I picture Nate.

Hunting me.

Chasing me.

Catching me.

Fucking me into the dirt.

The pleasure builds—harder, faster—spiraling out of control, and then, I break. The vibrations flood my body, and I move my hips. All thoughts disappear as I allow myself to sink fully into the sensations. The toy thrums against that perfect spot inside of me, and my cries get louder as I push myself over the edge, screaming out in ecstasy as every muscle in my body clenches and my nerve endings set me alight. I open my eyes, and my surroundings come back to me. I take in my position and chuckle nervously when I realize just how much of a show I might have put on for any passerby.

If just thinking about Nate makes me come that hard ...

Having him will *destroy* me.

Nate

Fuck, fuck, FUCK!

I'm going to die.

I am quite literally going to perish. This is every dream and every fantasy come true, and it's playing out in front of me.

Like always, I positioned myself outside Olivia's apartment—down the side and hidden from the street by trees. Usually, I don't get much. A glimpse of her moving around. Maybe nothing at all.

Tonight?

Tonight, she opened her curtains.

And then ...

She put on a fucking show.

I grip my cock, pumping desperately as I watch her fall apart. Her sweat-slicked skin. The way her mouth falls open when she moans. The pink vibrator. I nearly come when she spreads her legs wider, giving me a perfect view. I fumble for my phone, snapping a picture. It's blurry—shaky—but I don't care.

I need to remember this.

She's so close now. Her cries are building—higher, faster Her body trembling—*just like I knew it would.*

I'm barely breathing as I take in the sheen of sweat on her brow, her mussed hair, and the shape of her mouth as she cries out. I move my fist at a punishing pace—slightly too tight to be comfortable, but I've lost control. I almost black out as my release crashes over me and ropes of cum spurt from my tip, coating my hand, my pants, and the grass in front of me. Seconds later, Olivia screams, and I watch in awe as her body tenses before relaxing, a satisfied smile on her face.

After taking a few moments to compose herself, she rises from the sofa and closes the curtains, barring my sight again. I release a low moan and tuck my still-hard cock back into my pants, knowing that I'm likely going to be fucking my fist a few more times before the night is over. I will never forget this.

Nate

My phone ringing jolts me awake, dragging me from a restless sleep. I curse, fumbling to answer without even checking the caller ID.

"Nate," rings a voice as familiar to me as my own.

"Mom? Why are you calling so early? What's wrong?" I always talk with Mom, but, like me, she's not a morning person.

"He's out," she whispers.

The world tilts beneath me.

I go *cold*.

I can hear Mom's shaky breathing through the phone.

"What do you mean, he's out? I thought he still had a couple more years?"

"He got parole."

"Fuck!" I yell, thrusting my hand out and knocking a glass off my nightstand, feeling satisfaction in the shattering of glass. I'm up off the bed instantly and my mind races with what I could do to protect her.

"When?" I snarl, already pacing, my hands clenched into fists.

"A few weeks ago," she admits. "I know you're worried, but I have the restraining order. If he breaches it, he'll end up right back in prison."

"Mom, that doesn't mean shit, and you know it." My vision blurs with rage. "You should've called me the second you found out."

"I didn't want to stress you."

"I don't trust him," I snap. "He's unhinged. What if he—"

"He won't," she interrupts gently.

"Maybe I need to come stay with you for a while." Mom doesn't live far away—only in Jefferson, and the thought of leaving her unprotected while her abusive fucker of an ex could find her at any time makes me feel sick to my stomach.

"Don't be stupid, Nate. There's no reason to do that. I'll be fine, but I'll call you if anything suspicious happens. Okay?"

My hands shake, and I resist the urge to break more things. "I don't like it," I growl.

"Neither do I, but we will handle it."

I scoff. "Yeah, alright. Love you, Mom."

"Love you, too."

I end the call and throw my fist into the wall. Shooting pain lances through my knuckles as the plaster crumbles beneath my fist. It's satisfying, but not as satisfying as putting my fist through his head. I sit on the edge of my bed and rest my head in my hands, running my fingers through my hair and pulling at the strands.

Darren. Fucking Darren.

He spent the last four years rotting in prison—exactly where he belongs.

For years, my mother hid what he did to her. The bruises. The broken ribs. The fear. I should've known. Should've seen the signs. But I didn't.

When I finally did—when I walked in and saw him cornering her with a knife—I nearly killed him. I wanted to—god, I wanted to. It was only Mom's terror, and the pain from her injuries, that kept me sane enough to hold back. Instead, I poured every bit of myself into ensuring he got locked up and wasn't able to hurt her again.

He shouldn't be out. The idea that he somehow managed to get out on parole is disgusting, and I'm horrified that it took so long for someone to notify my mom. Anything could have happened to her in these last few weeks. Everyone knows that restraining orders don't do shit if the person it's against is unhinged. And anyone who could beat up someone as sweet as my mother so badly that she needed physical therapy to recover from her injuries is more than unhinged.

I'm breathing heavily, my face hot, as rage boils my blood and fear threatens to overwhelm me. The thought of seeing Mom in a position like that again is paralyzing. She might not want me to come and stay with her, but I sure as hell will be checking on her all the time. And if there is even the slightest whiff of Darren in Jefferson or here in New Orleans, I'm going to do whatever I can to make sure he rots in prison.

The only thing that stops me from going completely off the rails is the fact that I have another session with Olivia today. Since the night at her apartment, she's been my only focus.

And I won't let Darren take this from me.

"Little devil, little devil," I murmur, pressing her against the wall. "You are too tempting for words."

She doesn't push me away. She tilts her head up, lips slightly parted, bright blue eyes locked on mine—innocent and sinful all at once. But she's not innocent. And she knows it. When I stepped into her office and saw what she was wearing, every other thought—Darren, my mom, everything—vanished. There is only her.

Her chest rises and falls rapidly, her breath unsteady as I lean in, trailing my tongue from her collarbone to the shell of her ear. A soft moan slips past her lips, her body shifting against mine, but I don't let her escape.

"Did you wear this tiny little skirt for me?" My fingers graze the hem, teasing. "It's positively indecent."

She tilts her hips forward, brushing against my aching length. "Maybe," she purrs.

I glance down at the fabric barely covering her, my fingers skimming over the tops of her thighs. She wore this for *me*.

It's all wrong for a professional setting and barely covers the globes of her ass. Add that to the no bra situation of our last session, and there's no doubt in my mind.

She's playing with fire.

And she *wants* to get burned.

"So, what if I did?" she taunts. "What are you going to do about it?" I rock my hips forward, and we groan together as my cock presses between her legs. "I looked at that Hunted chat room you told me about," she gasps as my hands trail the hem of her skirt.

"Did you now?" I murmur, stroking my fingers up the inside of her leg. "And what did you find, little devil?"

She shudders as I move beneath her skirt, tracing smooth skin—higher, higher.

Then my fingers reach her heat.

Bare.

No underwear.

I curse, my control slipping.

"Fuck." My hand tightens on her thigh, my other gripping her hip, forcing her still as I hitch up her skirt to bare her to me.

"Hunter N-eight," she whispers, breathing hard but making no motion to stop my actions. I barely catch her words, so entranced by her beautiful pussy, bared and glistening pink. My fingers halt, my grip tightening slightly. I drag my gaze to hers, my pulse out of control.

She knows.

She fucking knows.

Her pupils are blown, her body flushed, her hands clutching at me instead of pushing away.

Not fear.

Want.

"Am I her?" she whispers.

Her.

My obsession. My secret. The reason my blood has been boiling for weeks, my hands aching to claim, my mind consumed with nothing but her. She's figured it out—and she isn't running.

She wants this.

Something inside me shatters. Instead of answering, I crash my mouth to hers. The back of her head hits the wall as I push myself harder against her so that I can feel every inch of her warm body. Her lips move with mine, forceful and punishing, as she fights for dominance with her tongue, as I capture every noise she makes.

Her hands reach my back and slide up my t-shirt to feel my skin beneath. Her nails graze a path up and down before moving to my front, where she fumbles with the button on my jeans.

I grab her wrists, pinning them above her head. "Not so fast, little devil," I growl against her lips. She whimpers, hips rolling against me, the heat of her bare pussy pressing against the bulge in my jeans. "How soundproof is this room?" I murmur.

"I—I don't know," she gasps.

I smirk. "Guess I'll have to keep you quiet, then."

I place both of my hands to cup her ass and, with one movement, lift her. She wraps her legs around me just as I want. I use the leverage of the wall to help hold her as I reach down to free my aching cock from my pants. Precum dribbles down my length, as desperate for her as my heart.

I fist myself, running the head through her soaking folds, teasing her, making her squirm. Her head tilts back against the wall, her lips parting on a shaky breath. "Tell me you want this," I demand.

Her hands flex in my grip, her thighs tightening around me.

"I want it," she breathes.

I thrust inside her in one stroke. She cries out, and I devour the sound, sealing my mouth to hers as I drive deeper. Her heels dig into my lower back, and I become frustrated with the bunched-up clothing that she wears, acting as a barrier between my flesh and hers.

I'm going to fuck her here, nice and hard.

Then I'm going to take her home and bury myself in her over and over again until she can't remember her own name.

Olivia

"**N**ate," I gasp against his lips as his hips piston into me, over and over.

My wrists are pinned above my head, keeping me at his mercy—and fuck, I love it. I want to touch him, to dig my nails into his back, but being trapped beneath him is somehow even better. His mouth leaves mine, moving down my neck, nipping and sucking a path to my collarbone.

Then—

A sharp bite.

I hiss, the sting morphing into a moan as he soothes the spot with his tongue before biting again.

"Shh. You don't want Sophia to come barging in now do you?" Nate whispers, his voice dark with hunger. I bite down hard on my lip to stop myself from crying out as he slams into me.

So deep.

So good.

I taste the coppery, metallic taste of blood and realize I bit harder than I meant to. Nate pulls back slightly and stares at my lips with unabashed desire. He leans, licks across my bloody lip, and groans at the taste.

Fuck. Why is that so hot?

"You take me so well," he growls, thrusting deeper. "So warm, so tight. I knew the second I saw you"—his fingers tighten around my wrists—"that you belonged to me."

I spiral toward release, my body tensing and trembling.

"That's it," he hisses, pace unrelenting. "Squeeze my cock. Milk me dry."

Pleasure crashes over me, my thighs shaking, my core tightening as I come hard. I bite into Nate's neck to keep from screaming, and he groans, his thrusts turning wild before he slams deep and spills inside me. Heat floods my throbbing core, and my limbs turn to jelly. He doesn't lower me immediately. His hands stay firm, holding me close, chests rising and falling together.

Breathless.

His fingers trail over my face—my cheek, my jaw, my lips. I don't think I've ever felt this ... wanted. Maybe it's the danger. Maybe it's the risk of being caught.

Or maybe ...

It's just him.

Finally, his cock softens, and he gently unwraps my legs from his waist. As he pulls out, warmth spills down my thigh. His gaze darkens, locked on the slick mess he left behind. He drops to his knees, and my breath catches.

Nate slides two fingers up my inner thigh, collecting his cum, then pushes it back inside me. I whimper. The sensitivity is overwhelming; the sheer depravity of his actions twists something dark inside me.

But I don't stop him. I don't *want* to stop him.

"That's it, little devil," he murmurs, his voice thick with satisfaction. "Now you're gonna sit through your next session full of me." I shudder. "You'll feel it—my cum dripping down your thighs—and you'll think about me the entire time. Won't you?"

I nod, unable to form words.

He smirks. "Good girl. I'm going to meet you outside at the end of the day, and you're going to come home with me." Not a question. A demand. And again, I nod. "I'm going to go because you'll need a few minutes to make yourself presentable again." He winks and pulls my skirt back down to cover me. He traces my neck, and I assume he's looking at the marks he made. "These might need covering."

Then he's gone, and I'm left standing there, thighs slick, shaking, praying the day goes by quickly so I can have more of him.

Practicing therapy while being unable to focus on anything besides the pool of cum between your legs is exactly as uncomfortable as you'd think it would be. If my clients noticed me squirming in my seat, then they didn't show it. But I know this can't continue. Now that Nate and I have fully crossed the line, I can't be professional with him. Not when I already know that one taste will never be enough.

By the time my last session ends, I can barely contain myself.

I practically run out the front door, eager to see if he is waiting for me like he said he would be. I glance around and find him leaning against the wall off to the side of my office building. His face lights up when he notices me, and I swear my heart skips a beat. How disgustingly sweet is that?

"Hey, little devil," he smirks. "How did I feel between your legs all afternoon?" I feel a blush creep over my skin, the reality of what we did hitting harder now that we are out in the open.

"I think we need to have a conversation," I tell him, sure that firing him as a client is the right thing to do. His expression doesn't change. He nods as if he's been expecting this.

"Would you like to have dinner with me?"

I hesitate for only a second. "I'd like that," I murmur shyly like I didn't just have this man fuck me against the wall mere hours ago.

He reached for my hand, and I let him take it. For the first time since meeting him, he seems uncertain.

And for the first time since I've met him, I've never been more.

Olivia

"Tell me more about yourself," Nate says, eyes fixed on me as he leans forward.

He's brought me to a small, cozy pizza joint near my office, and I can't help but wonder if he chose this place intentionally. Because if he knows me as well as I think he does, then he knows my weakness for cheesy, greasy pizza. Which makes me wonder: how much else does he already know?

Then it hits me. "Oh my god," I blurt out. "You sent me the pug mug!"

His fingers fidget against the table, but a sheepish smile tugs at his lips. "Uh ... yeah," he admits, rubbing the back of his neck. "Did you like it?"

"It was adorable. But not knowing who sent it was ... unsettling. Now that I do?" I tilt my head, studying him. "I love it even more."

His smile brightens. "Figures," I murmur. "You already knew I love pugs, didn't you?"

"I've done my research," he teases. "Doug the pug, right?"

I laugh, shaking my head. He really does know everything. "Okay," I challenge, leaning in. "Instead of me telling you about myself, why don't you tell me what you already know?"

Nate grins. "I know you're thirty-two. Grew up in Texas with your mom, dad, and baby sister, Tia. You moved out for college, then settled in New Orleans after graduating."

I nod. So far, all correct.

"Your favorite animal is a pug. Favorite food? Pizza—extra cheesy, no pineapple. You wear your hair down for work but always put it up the second you're off-duty. And you like your coffee as sweet as humanly possible."

He smirks. "How am I doing?"

I blink, impressed. "You weren't kidding about doing your research."

His expression turns smug. "Anything you don't know?" I press.

For the first time, he pauses. "I guess ..." he hesitates, tilting his head. "I don't know why you're still single."

The question makes heat creep up my neck. I reach for my drink, stalling.

"I couldn't find much about your dating history," he adds, studying my reaction.

I swallow, debating how much I should say. Finally, I exhale. "I didn't date much in college. I was focused on my studies. And, after that ... well ..."

I bite my lip, debating whether to continue. But he's been open with me. And deep down, I want him to know. I lift my gaze to meet his. "I've never really found anyone who satisfies me."

His brows raise slightly, intrigue sparking in his dark eyes.

"... Sexually," I clarify, my voice lower now.

The corner of his mouth twitches upward, but he says nothing—watches me, waiting.

I shift in my seat, pushing forward. "The men I've been with were ... boring. I didn't know exactly what I needed, but I knew that whatever they gave me wasn't it. It barely scratched the itch—always left me wanting more."

Nate reaches out, fingers brushing mine, locking our hands on the table. "And what do you think about me?" His thumb strokes my palm. "Do I do more than just ... scratch the itch?"

I swallow hard. "Yes," I breathe.

His grin grows wider. "Great. Glad we sorted that out."

The spell breaks instantly, and I shake my head, biting back a laugh. But his teasing only serves as a reminder of why we're here. Why we aren't at home. Why he isn't buried deep inside me right now.

I take a steadying breath. "I can't see you as a client anymore." The words come fast, spilling before I lose my nerve. "It's too dangerous. We could've been caught today, and my career would be over. I've worked too hard to risk that."

He nods. "Okay."

I blink. "That's it?"

"I mean ... yeah. Makes sense." He shrugs.

"I can refer you to another therapist—"

"Nah," he interrupts with a laugh. "Not necessary. I was only there for you. And if you're willing to keep seeing me?" His smirk returns. "Then I don't need therapy. Not sure we did too much of that anyway." He winks.

I groan. Why is he like this? Desperate to shift the conversation, I reach for the first question that comes to mind. "How's your mom?"

The change in his expression is instant. The lightness disappears. His smile fades. And his hand slips from mine.

My stomach tightens. "Nate?" His jaw clenches. "What is it? Is she okay?" For a long moment, he doesn't answer.

When he finally speaks, his voice is low. Tense. "My mom was in a bad relationship a few years back. Guy named Darren." He exhales sharply. "I didn't realize how bad it was until she was nearly broken. He was hurting her badly. And often."

My chest tightens. I reach out on instinct, my hand covering his. He's right, I was a shit therapist for him. But I saw—I know—how deeply he loves his mother. And now? I can see how much this is eating him alive.

"I did everything I could to put him in prison," he says. "And I thought that was it. We moved on. She was safe." His voice dips even lower. "But he's out." My breath catches. He shakes his head, frustration evident. "I just found out. And I don't know what he's thinking or planning. But I do know he's dangerous. And if he comes near her again ..." His fists clench against the table.

I squeeze his hand. "Oh, Nate," I whisper. "That's awful. How scary for you and your mom. What can you do? Does she live close?"

"She's in Jefferson," he mutters. "Not far. But there's nothing I can do except keep my eyes open. Wait for her to see something. And then ..." He doesn't finish the sentence. He doesn't have to.

Before I can say more, our server appears with steaming hot pizza, setting it between us. I exhale, letting the subject drop—for now. Instead, I grab a slice, moaning at the first bite. Nate chuckles, eyes heating.

"Thanks for ordering no pineapple," I say between mouthfuls.

"Of course," he smirks. "Pineapple doesn't belong on pizza."

I gasp, pointing at him. "Yes! Exactly!"

He grins. "Did I just win your heart over pineapple hatred?"

"Honestly?" I chew, pretending to consider. "Maybe."

And just like that, the tension eases. As the night progresses, I'm surprised just how comfortable I feel with him. Given our ... *unusual* introduction, we can skip a lot of the small talk and jump in a little deeper. He knows a lot about me from his "research", and I know a bit about him from therapy. Unorthodox for sure, but, hey, it seems to be working for us.

We don't delve back into the conversation about his mom, and I get the impression that he's trying to suppress his fear. I have a strong urge to comfort him—or perhaps distract him. As we finish our pizza, I start to fidget in my seat. I rub my thighs together, and my skin heats. Now that we've talked and gotten to know each other more personally, I'm thinking about what's next. I wonder if he's thinking the same thing.

Nate smirks as he notices me changing my sitting position for the tenth time in as many minutes. "Do you want to come back to my apartment?" He asks, and I nod far too eagerly.

I want nothing more.

Nate

I drive Olivia back to my apartment, and the question escapes me before I can hold it back. "Do you not care that I've been following you for months? How do you know I'm not a serial killer?"

She glances at me, her lips curving into the faintest smirk. "Are you a serial killer?"

"Of course not."

She laughs, a soft, melodic sound that wraps around me. I want to hear it on repeat. "I'm pretty sure that's exactly what a serial killer would say," she teases.

"Fair point. But why do you feel so safe around me?" I don't know why I'm pushing this, why I need to hear her say it. Maybe I still don't believe it myself—that she wants me and isn't running. A normal person would not be on board for that, but somehow, she doesn't seem put off.

She bites her lip and pauses before answering. "I don't know. I consider myself a good judge of character. I can usually tell when a client is high risk or someone is not completely genuine with me. Even when you weren't telling me your whole truth in therapy, I felt you were being open and honest. You haven't hurt me or tried to force me into anything. Everything between us has been consensual. And I just don't feel you're a bad guy."

"I've done some bad things in the past," I admit reluctantly.

"So have I," she responds. "But as long as you haven't murdered anyone, raped anyone, or have the FBI hunting you, I'm willing to give this a shot. I know stalking can be dangerous, but ... I don't know. The idea of it? It turns me on. I don't know what that says about me, but I'm done questioning it."

"I guess, I'm done questioning it too, then," I say with a smile, meeting her dark eyes.

The moment we walk into my apartment building, she's on me. She grabs my face and pulls it down to hers, pressing our lips together and running her tongue along the seam of my lips so I open for her. I fumble with my keys, struggling to unlock the door as she trails kisses and small bites down my neck, her hands slipping beneath my shirt, dragging across my stomach. I'm so shocked by her brazen display of lust that I can barely function, but somehow, I manage to get us inside.

Without hesitation, Olivia lifts her blouse over her head, displaying the deep red bralette underneath. She grabs a fistful of my shirt and pulls me forward.

"Where's the bedroom?" she asks huskily. I'm surprised and thrilled by her dominance but now that my shock is wearing off, it's time for me to take control.

I yank her skirt down in one swift motion and groan when I realize. "Still no underwear?"

She smirks. "Figured it'd save time."

Jesus.

I scoop her up, her legs wrapping around my waist like she belongs there; like this is exactly where she was always meant to be. I move us toward the bedroom, fighting against my basest instincts. I need to slow down. Do this properly.

"Limits," I pant against her lips. "We need to discuss limits."

"No limits."

My cock twitches violently. Fuck, she has no idea what she's unleashing. "Safe word," I grunt out, throwing her on the bed so her pussy is completely exposed and open for me.

"Pineapple," she says with a smile, and I laugh.

"Okay, so if I do anything that makes you uncomfortable, you'll say pineapple? Are you on birth control?"

"Don't you think you should have asked me that a few hours ago?" Shit, yeah, she's right. I haven't been very logical or safe, but I'm trying now. "I have an IUD and my last test was clear," she states, and my breath leaves me in a whoosh of relief.

"Mine too," I tell her.

"Nate, please fuck me," she begs.

With pleasure.

I undress while Olivia unhooks her bra, slipping it off her delicate shoulders. This is the first time I've seen her completely undressed, and my brain tries to short-circuit. Her dusty rose nipples are hardened into points, and her hair is splayed out around her like a halo. But she's no angel. She's my undoing, my temptation, my little devil. One that I'd willingly sell my soul to.

I rifle through my nightstand until I find what I'm looking for, and then crawl onto the bed so I'm resting between her legs. "I'm going to tie you to the bed, little devil," I tell her, and her breathing hitches.

I loop silk ties around her wrists, fastening them to my headboard. I tug once, making sure they're snug but not too tight. "Too much?" I check, brushing my fingers over her skin.

She shakes her head. "More."

"What do you like?" I press a slow, lingering kiss to her throat, trailing lower, sucking a nipple into my mouth.

She gasps and arches her back, pressing into me. "I-I don't know. Rough. I think I like rough."

My lips curve into a slow, wicked smirk. "You think?" She nods again, her pupils blown wide.

I sit back, fisting my cock in one hand, stroking lazily as I take in the sight of her. I have her completely naked and at my mercy, tied to my bed and aching with need. I know I need to make this last, but I can't help giving myself a few hard strokes while I look down at the goddess before me. Her deep brown eyes—pupils dilated—watch me with interest as she licks her lips.

"Are you wet for me, little devil?" I ask, and she nods her head vigorously. "Let's see."

I spread her thighs wider, trailing my fingers down the soft skin of her inner thighs. I slide them through her slick folds and groan.

"Mm, perfect." I bring my fingers to my mouth and lick them, savoring her delicious taste and knowing that I'm going to need more.

She whimpers as I insert a finger inside her, brushing her walls and watching her squirm. I add another, and her breathing becomes heavier, her legs quivering. I lean over her to suck on her breast again, playing with that taut nipple with my tongue and teeth. I thrust my fingers harder, faster, determined to wring out as many orgasms from her as possible before I inevitably explode.

A few more pumps of my fingers, and she's coming all over my hand with a scream. "You come so beautifully for me, my good girl," I praise, and she looks at me through hooded eyes. But I barely give her a moment of reprieve. She's still trembling when I slide lower, pressing a kiss to her belly.

"Wha-what are you—"

Before she can finish, I bury my face between her legs.

She jolts. "Nate!"

Her thighs clamp around my shoulders, her body locking up as my tongue flicks over her clit. I don't stop. I don't even slow down. She tastes like fucking heaven.

I can't breathe, but, fuck, what a way to go. My tongue circles her clit, and my fingers find their place back inside her wet heat. I want to live between her thighs, feasting on her like she's my last meal on this earth. I want her cries and whimpers of desire to be the only thing I hear for the rest of time.

Olivia

"Nate!" I gasp as my thighs grip him tighter and my hands pull at my restraints, desperate to touch him. He's relentless, barely giving me a break after one orgasm before he has me careening towards the next. The words coming out of my mouth are an incoherent, jumbled mess, and all I can focus on is the electricity flowing through my nerves, burning me alive in the best way possible. His stubble creates delicious friction, and the sting of pain as he stretches me with another finger is exquisite.

I shatter when he bites down on my clit—not too hard, but precisely what I need. My back bows, muscles locking up as my climax rips through me. I cry out his name again, loud and raw. Tired and sweaty, I release my hold on his head, worried that I've suffocated him. He looks at me, eyes shining and my release coating his mouth. How can I still want him this much after two orgasms? But he hasn't finished, so he isn't finished with me. That horny little devil on my shoulder has taken the wheel today, and I can't get enough of this sexy-as-fuck man.

Nate moves from between my legs to the headboard and gently releases my hands. I circle my wrists to restore blood flow before reaching down to hold his thick cock in my hand. He's slick with precum, and as I move my hand up and down his shaft, he closes his eyes and leans his head back, letting out a guttural groan.

"I've been dreaming about this," he tells me. "Every day, every night, I dream about what it would be like to touch you, to have you touch me. You can't even imagine how often I've come over the fantasy. But this is better than I ever could have imagined." Warmth pools in my core at his reverence, his obsession. "I need you to roll over onto your hands and knees and stick that perky ass out for me."

I eagerly do as he says and wait patiently for him to make his next move. Without warning, a loud *slap* rings through the air and my muscles tense at the impact of his hand against my ass. It stings, but in a way that has me wanting more.

"More," I gasp.

Slap, slap, slap. Three more lashes fall against my ass cheek, and with each one, my moans get louder, my pussy gets wetter, and my need for him gets stronger. I cry out when he bites down on the already tender flesh. Pain lances through me, but with surprise, I realize that the pain already has me on the edge of release. I don't want gentle. I don't want soft. I want this. I want someone unafraid to hurt me, to make me feel everything.

I scream when he finally thrusts into me, stretching me wide.

My back bows, my face pressing into the mattress. "Good girl," he growls, and fuck, the praise nearly pushes me over the edge.

His hips piston into me, hard and fast with no reprieve. I can't catch my breath. All I'm capable of doing is holding onto the sheets with white knuckles while the sounds of the headboard thumping against the wall and our breaths and moans entwine together in an erotic symphony. Nate's thrusts pause, and I whimper at the loss of movement.

"Has anyone ever taken you here?" His finger circles my tightest hole, teasing. I nod. His snarl is pure, primal fury.

"From now on, all of this is mine. Do you hear me? You're mine. No one else gets to touch you again." The possessiveness is just another red flag to add to his flagpole but once again, what should make me want to run, has the complete opposite effect on my horny bitch of a brain.

"Yours," I whisper, and he responds by pushing deep into me once more, causing me to cry out in surprise.

I feel the sensation of something wet landing on my hole and realize that it's his spit. As he continues his punishing pace, he uses his saliva in place of lube and inserts a finger. I squirm as the added intrusion enhances the feeling of fullness. He works me open and adds another finger. I'm panting, desperate to come.

"Time to come for me, little devil," Nate says, pumping me with both his cock and his fingers until I detonate. My cries come out more like a wail as I'm thrown over the edge to oblivion. Nate growls loudly, and his body twitches as he comes inside of me.

He collapses forward, his muscular chest pressing mine firmly into the bed. With ragged breaths and sweaty bodies, we soak up the moment of intimacy as we come down from our releases.

"Fuck Livi, you're everything I could have ever dreamed of and more."

Livi.

I shiver. No one has ever called me that before. I love it just as much as I love "little devil".

With a grunt, he presses up on his hands and gently pulls out of me. We both roll onto our sides to face each other, and I already miss the feeling of his body. "Was that okay?" he asks, and I grin.

"Eh, I suppose it was okay," I deadpan. His eyes widen, looking genuinely offended. "It was everything," I snicker.

He relaxes, his lips curving into a slow, satisfied smile. "You're everything."

I stay still and watch Nate move from the bed into the adjoining bathroom. I take in the muscles of his back and his firm ass and … god damn, he's hot. He returns moments later with a warm washcloth and gently washes between my legs in silence. He rolls me back onto my stomach and takes care massaging my ass that still slightly stings from his lashes. He places soft kisses on both of my ass cheeks before positioning me to lie with my head on his chest.

His dick is still hard, and I marvel at his refractory period. He notices me looking and chuckles. "Don't worry, Livi. I'll be taking you again very soon, but right now, I just want to rest here with you." I nod and close my eyes, the thumping of his heart lulling me to sleep.

I spend the night at Nate's, and true to his word, not much sleep occurs. He's almost desperate in his need to take me, committing every inch of my body to memory as if he might wake up and I'd have disappeared. Not that I'm complaining. I've not been this deliciously sore from sex in all my life.

We finally passed out in the early morning hours, and as I wake, I find that I don't want to leave him to go to work. As I gradually regain consciousness, I become aware of our entangled limbs and his soft breaths tickling my neck. I open my eyes and take in the softness of his face in sleep. His warm brown hair shines almost golden in the rays of light that filter through the curtains. Careful not to wake him up, I run a hand over his rough stubble that I felt against my skin throughout the night, remembering the bite of it between my legs as it added to the already heightened sensations. The facial hair makes him look harsher than he is, but I've seen glimpses of playfulness intertwined with the intensity of his obsession.

His eyelids flutter open, and I'm drawn into his deep brown eyes. His lips turn up in a sleepy smile, and he wraps an arm around me, bringing me closer. "Good morning, little devil. Were you watching me sleep?" He murmurs in my ear. "That's kind of stalkerish behavior, you know."

"Pot calling the kettle black, don't you think?" I respond with a laugh. "Ugh, what time is it? I have to go to work," I groan as I reluctantly unstick myself from his body.

Nate reaches over to his phone on the nightstand reminding me that, at some point between arriving at his home and him fucking my brains out, I've misplaced my own. "It's still early, only seven a.m.."

"No wonder I'm still so tired. I swear we only got to sleep a couple of hours ago."

"Yeah, I'm sure that's the only reason," he replies with a wiggle of his eyebrows, causing me to snort.

"Shower?" he asks, and I nod enthusiastically. Although he made an effort to clean me up after each round as his form of aftercare, I still desperately need a shower.

Nate shows me more of his attentive and caring side as we shower together. Okay, I still got down on my knees and sucked his cock until he was screaming out my name and coming down my throat, but after that, he washed my body and my hair for me. It was intimate, and the gesture felt important. No one has cared for me like this before. My insides churn with feelings I'm unfamiliar with. While surprising, my physical reactions to him aren't that concerning to me; however, these emotional ones are far more terrifying. I shouldn't be feeling like this about someone I just met, but when I gaze into his adoring eyes, I fear that I'm jumping off a cliff and free-falling into the unknown.

Olivia

I finish my notes with Nate on my mind and the thoughts of him providing me with far too many distractions. It means my notes took longer to write than usual, and I'm frustrated with myself for falling behind. After leaving Nate's apartment this morning, I raced back home to change. Nothing says 'walk of shame' like entering the office wearing the same crinkled outfit as the previous day. I'm usually very put together, so Sophia would be suspicious. However, the redness of my eyes from stupidly falling asleep with my contacts in led to some questions.

I pack up my desk and gather my things to leave when a knock on my office door startles me.

"Olivia, someone delivered some mail for you. It came by courier rather than by post, and says confidential on the front, so I haven't opened it," Sophia says, poking her head in. I thank her and take the large envelope from her before saying goodbye and telling her

I'll close up.

I hear her leave and decide to open the envelope rather than wait until tomorrow. It's probably legal, and I want to know what I'll likely have to deal with tomorrow. The envelope contains a small stack of printed photographs. Confused, I pull them out, and my heart plummets when I see what they contain.

The first photo shows my office, me in my usual chair, and Nate leaning down over me with his lips against my neck. My eyes are closed, my head thrown back, with a smile. The next is a photo of Nate holding me up against the wall, my arms above my head, and my skirt bunched around my waist. Nate's body blocks most of the indecency, but it's clear what is happening.

The first thought that enters my mind is that Nate might have done this as part of his obsessive behavior, a bit of a game. But I quickly disregard the thought because, after last night, it just doesn't seem like something he would do. Maybe he might have initially, when he was still secretly my stalker, but things changed yesterday. Surely, he would know that this would scare me.

My heart races, and my pulse thrums in my ears as I'm left with so many questions: who did this? How did they do this? And most of all, why did they do this?

I'm in so much fucking trouble. My breaths shorten, and I struggle to inhale enough oxygen. I'm going to lose my job. I'm going to lose everything. I flip through the rest of the photos and see more of the same kinds of images, all from Nate's sessions with me. The last photo is not a photo at all, but a note:

Naughty, naughty Olivia

I don't know how long I stare at the note before panic drives me to race around my office, looking for a hidden camera—anything that might explain how this happened. I pull pictures off my walls, move the furniture around, and look over every surface. There's nothing. Unless the person was using some high-tech micro camera, whatever was used to take those photos is gone now.

Eventually, I admit defeat and leave the office. Nate already messaged me to say that he would be meeting me at my apartment tonight, having put my number in his phone this morning. I'm grateful that I will be seeing him—after all, this affects him too. Not even close to the same extent, but he needs to know.

Nate is already out the front of my building, waiting for me, and without thought, I throw myself into his arms. My panic still hasn't subsided, and he catches onto my disheveled appearance. He places his hands on my shoulders and holds me away from him as he looks into my eyes, as if he can see my soul.

"What's wrong?" he asks worriedly.

"Inside," I tell him, leading him to my door. I fumble with my keys, my hands shaking slightly from the stress. He steadies me with his hands, and I collapse onto the sofa when we enter the apartment.

"Livi, you're worrying me. What's going on?" I pull the envelope out of my bag and hand him the photos. He flips through them in silence, his face devoid of emotion.

"What the actual fuck?" he yells, throwing the photos across the room. I don't move, unsure of what to say. He grips my face in his hands. "Tell me what's going on."

"I don't know," I whisper, my eyes filling with tears. Nate's face softens, and his hold on my face loosens. "They were delivered to my office right before I left tonight."

"Did anyone else see them?" he asks quickly.

"No, the envelope was still sealed when Sophia gave it to me. She said a courier delivered it."

"Do you have any clients that may have done this?"

"Apart from you …" I say hesitantly. He growls in response, and I try to backtrack. "I mean, I thought at first, maybe … but I don't think it was you."

"It sure as fuck wasn't me. I never wanted to scare you. Any photos I took were for my personal use, and I would *never* share them with anyone else." I process his words and decide to come back to that later. I can only deal with one stalker taking photos of me at a time.

"What do they want from me? There's no threat; they aren't asking me for anything. It's like a warning, but I don't know what they want," I exclaim, hysteria bubbling. I knew messing around with a client was a bad fucking idea, but now, faced with the potential repercussions of my actions, I'm so damn angry with myself for getting into this situation in the first place.

Nate pulls me into his arms, but I push him away. I can't help feeling angry towards him, too. Logically, I know that as the professional in the relationship, the blame lies with me, but right now, I'm not thinking straight. Nate's eyes flash with hurt at the dismissal, but he gives me space as I start to pace around the room.

"It's going to be okay, little devil. We will figure this out. You've already fired me as a client so nothing like this will happen again," Nate says softly, calmly, like he's trying to soothe a frightened animal.

My erratic heartbeat starts to slow, and I'm finally able to suck in a lungful of air. I can get through this. I can figure out what they want and keep my reputation clean. My feet stop moving, and I'm hit with a wave of exhaustion. Nate comes close to me again, opening his arms in invitation. This time, I fall into them and allow him to offer me reassurance and support.

"There's nothing we can do right now," he tells me, and I know he's right. "Let's watch some trash TV and then have an early night, and we can start fresh tomorrow." I nod, my head still firmly pressed to his chest.

Later, we crawl into bed together, and I lay my head on Nate's chest, listening to the heavy thud of his heart. All the anger from earlier has dissipated, but I'm left with a numbness that's taken over my mind and body.

Nate

It's late. I should be asleep, but there's no way in hell that I can rest knowing that someone is out to get Olivia. *My* Olivia. Her head rests on my chest, and soft snores fill the air. I stare down at her, my feelings alternating between marveling at the reality of having her in my arms, and the primal rage of wanting to kill anyone who means her harm.

The longer I think about the photos, the more I wonder if this has anything to do with Darren. It seems like a big jump, but it's suspicious that something like this would happen not long after he was released from prison. I assumed he would go after Mom, but he fucking *hates* me. I'm the one who ruined his pathetic excuse of a life, after all. But why would he target Olivia? How does he even know about Olivia? This theory makes no sense and a lot of sense simultaneously, and I've been driving myself crazy, going around in circles, with my thoughts all night. Maybe this has nothing to do with Darren at all, maybe I'm just being paranoid. One thing's for sure: I won't let anyone hurt what belongs to me.

Somehow, I manage to drift off to sleep in the early hours of the morning, and I'm woken up to the heavenly sensation of a hand around my cock. And for once, it's not mine! I smile and open my eyes to see a sleep-mussed Olivia, staring at me intently as she moves her fist up and down.

"How are you doing, beautiful?" I ask, my words finishing on a low moan as she squeezes.

"I have to get ready for work soon, and right now, I just want to forget what's happening. Please help me forget." She doesn't have to ask twice. I'd give her the world if she asked for it. I roll her onto her back and position my body on top of hers. In one movement, I slide myself into her warm heat, and a soft sigh escapes her lips. We stay in this position, bodies pressed together, holding each other's gaze as I thrust into her slowly. I take my time, wanting to show her every bit of care I possess. There will be time to satisfy our more adventurous needs later, but right now, I want her to know I'm here. I'm her protector.

Her climax builds and builds before she tumbles over the edge, pulling me with her, and still, we don't break eye contact.

"Thank you," she whispers.

After a few moments, I roll off her. Dread hangs over us, and I know she's afraid of what might happen. Her career is on the line, and I won't tell her this yet, but I also worry that her safety is at risk. I vow to do what I can to keep her safe, and god help the person responsible for this if I find out who they are.

The next few days go by without any other ominous threats, but we are both still on edge. I find myself unwilling to let her too far out of my sight, afraid of what could happen if I do. The suspicion that Darren is somehow involved in this hasn't dissipated. My gut tells me something is wrong, and I can't fully relax when there's the slightest chance she's in danger.

Fortunately, Olivia seems to want me around as much as I want to be there. We have to part when she goes to the office, but where I used to go back home to work during the day, I now sit at a coffee shop across the road to monitor the entrance to her building. It makes me feel better to be close by, and it also offers her some comfort.

Saturday is spent together, holed up in her apartment, both of us seeking comfort in the touch of the other. We watch TV and order takeout, and I can't help but laugh when Olivia pulls out a battered version of the board game Monopoly.

"Wanna play?" she asks me, and I smirk at her.

"Wanna lose?" I fire back. Her eyes light with determination, and I see the spark that had been extinguished the last few days catch alight once more. *There's my girl.*

"Oh, it's on," she laughs.

An hour later, I have to admit defeat. "Damn, how are you so good at this?" I groan as I hand over a large sum for landing on one of her hotels. *Again.*

"A board game loving family and far too much time on my hands," she replies, her wide smile warming my heart.

"Well, I'm officially bankrupt," I announce, and she fist pumps in celebration. I thought I knew so much about Olivia Kane. I'd researched her past, studied her present, and felt like I knew what she wanted for her future. But these last few days have made me realize that I only knew the surface level of Olivia. I still only saw the parts of her she allowed the world to see. Now she's letting me in, truly letting me in, and I'm surprised and delighted by what I'm finding.

I've heard from others on the Hunter chat that a person's dream is often better than the reality—that the picture we form in our mind is better. That couldn't be farther from the truth with Olivia. Every new part of her that she allows me to see makes her even more perfect to me. My fantasies didn't do her justice. Not even close.

Olivia didn't want to leave the safety of her apartment today, and I understand. This is a normal reaction to a stranger taking intimate photos of her. But tomorrow is market day, and going to the market is part of her routine. I mention as much to her, and she pinches her bottom lip between her teeth in worry.

"Do you think it's okay to go? What if I'm being followed?"

"The market is busy. Even if they were following you, they can't hurt you with all those people around. I'd kill anyone who tries." Her pupils dilate, and her tongue runs over her lip, and I'm secretly pleased that she seems to like my admission. "I think we should go. I'll stay by your side if it makes you feel safer. I think it's important to keep up with your life. Until we know what they want, hiding away isn't going to achieve anything."

She nods. "You're right," she sighs.

CHAPTER 15

Olivia

Nate's right, the market is busy. Of course, it is. It always is. Logically, I know I'm safe here, surrounded by everyone with Nate's firm grip on my hand. But my heart still pounds frantically, and I can't help my gaze from flitting around, looking for anything suspicious. The problem is, I have no idea what I'm even looking for.

Focusing on what I'm here for is difficult, but Nate is trying hard to keep me grounded. He points out various market stalls, drawing my attention to the sensations surrounding me. The sounds of the bustling crowd, the smells of the freshly baked treats that have me drooling, the bright display of assorted flowers, and the feel of my hand in his. All of it helps to bring me out of my head, but I still can't relax. I haven't bought anything, and I feel like I'm just walking around aimlessly.

"You're so tense, little devil," Nate says, leaning over so that his stubble tickles the shell of my ear as he talks.

"You don't say," I respond, rolling my eyes. He knows exactly why I'm so tense.

"I know something that will relieve that tension," he tells me, nipping my ear lobe with his teeth, not hard, but hard enough to make me jump in shock.

"And what might that be?" I ask, although I know where he's going with this.

"Orgasms," he says with a cocksure grin, and the excitement in his eyes has me barking out a surprised laugh.

"Do you want to play a game?"

"What kind of game?" I ask breathily.

"Well, the kind that ends in orgasms, of course."

"Here?" I squeak. "We can't."

"Sure, we can. I remember the way you lit up the first time I told you about Hunted and the type of interests people use it to pursue. Do you know how beautiful you are when your cheeks turn pink?" Fuck, he's right. I know exactly how I felt, thinking about what doing some of those things would be like. I wanted it desperately. I still do.

"What's the game?" I breathe.

"You're going to run, little devil. Not so fast to draw attention to yourself, but I'll give you two minutes to hide from me, and then the chase begins."

My blood heats and my heart jumps—this time with excitement rather than fear. "And what happens if you catch me?"

"Hmm, I think you'll want me to catch you," he replies, and

I rub my thighs together at the thought. The movement doesn't escape his notice, but he turns to face the other direction instead of saying something.

"Two minutes, Livi," he says, and my legs move before my brain catches up. I wind through the throng of people, heeding Nate's warning not to draw attention to myself. I keep my stride fast and determined, resisting the urge to break into a run, and instead, I look like someone in a hurry. No one looks at me twice; everyone seems to mind their own business.

As much as I want to find a good hiding place, he was right when he said I'd want him to catch me, so I don't want to make it too hard for him. I consider my options, knowing I can't just keep walking around the market. A small alleyway off to the side, just beyond the border of the market, catches my eye, and I head towards it.

The alley is empty of people but littered with empty crates and boxes. Perfect for hiding. I crouch down behind a stack of crates and wait. My pulse thuds in my ears, drowning out the sounds of the market, and my panties are wet with anticipation. A part of my brain tries to warn me that separating from the crowd was a terrible idea, but that part is quickly squashed by the lust that fills my body.

I don't know how long I wait—it could be seconds or min-utes—but eventually, the sound of heavy footsteps reaches my ears. "Found you, little devil," comes his growly voice. I don't move. He can't see me down here, and he's just guessing where I am. I'm not going to give myself away.

"Boo," he says, bursting around the corner of the crates and causing me to jump a foot in the air in surprise.

"Fuck," I squeal as he grabs me by the arm, pulling me to him.

"That was far too easy. I knew you wanted me to catch you," he says, holding me tighter. I squirm in a pathetic act of trying to escape, but both of us know I'm not even trying.

"Time for your punishment," he tells me, his voice deep and … fuck, he's sexy. He turns me to face the stack of crates with my back to him. "Hands on the crates," he demands, and I obey quickly, heat pooling in my core. "This pussy is mine."

I gasp as he lifts the hem of my sundress, and I quickly look around the alley to ensure no one can see us. It's still empty, and we are hidden from any passersby. I try to turn my brain off to give in to this moment. Fortunately, Nate reads my mind and manages to short circuit my brain with the touch of his fingers as they circle my clit. *Fuck.*

With his hand down the front of my underwear, my dress hitched up, and my hands placed firmly against the crates, I'm completely at his mercy and exactly where he wants me. He's torturously slow, moving his fingers through my arousal, barely applying any pressure to the bundle of nerves.

"Do you want more?" he whispers, and I nod frantically.

"Yes, more, I need more."

He laughs, "Good girl, tell me what you want. Do you want my thick fingers inside you, filling you up, stroking your inner walls?"

"Yes, fuck, yes. Nate, do it."

I cry out as he plunges two fingers inside of me, and he uses his other hand to cover my mouth. "Shh, little devil, you don't want anyone to hear. Mmm, you're so warm and wet for me." He doesn't hold back, using his fingers to stretch and taunt me before adding another finger and filling me so well. I'm already on the edge, and that's where he keeps me, drawing me closer and closer but never letting me topple over. He keeps his hand covering my mouth, and I pant behind it, sweat beading on my forehead.

This is torture.

This is cruel.

This is *bliss*.

He leans into me, kissing my neck. "This is your punishment for getting caught so easily. You don't get to come until I allow it. You get to feel the same desperation I felt before I knew you. When I wanted you but couldn't have you."

"Please," I beg, not ashamed in the slightest by the desperation that laces my voice. His fingers still, and I cry out, "No! Don't stop!"

"Please, what?" he teases.

"Please let me come. I need to. Please. Can't bear it any longer." My words come out almost incoherent.

"Because you asked so nicely." His fingers begin to thrust into me, hard and fast, and I know our game is over. With his thumb he presses down on my clit adding the external stimulation I need to fall apart completely. The edging he'd done before draws out my orgasm to the point where I can barely stand. He holds me through it, all the while whispering to me about how much of a good girl I was, and how perfect I am. A tear tracks down my cheek at the realization that all this time, this is what I've been missing in my life.

Before leaving the market, Nate leads me to the flower stall, where he buys me a bouquet of blue orchids. On the way back to my apartment, I can't wipe the smile off my face, all thoughts of danger completely gone from my mind.

Nate

God fucking damn it! Dread pools in my gut as I stare down at the envelope I just pulled out of my mailbox. All it says is my name and nothing else, and without even looking, I know the contents are something that I don't want to see.

Olivia hasn't received any other ominous threats from her stalker. As the days continued without incident, she started to relax and now seems to think that it was just a warning. She's still nervous but nowhere near as panicked as she was before.

I've still been on edge, something telling me that it's not over. There was no resolution, no explanation as to why this person felt the need to do what they did. I refuse to let it go. I've been doing everything I can to try and find information about Darren's whereabouts, but he seems to have gone quiet since his release. Nothing suspicious has happened to mom—thank fuck—but I still have this feeling that he is involved somehow.

Holding this envelope, I'm sure that whatever it contains is going to throw us into a tailspin, that our couple of weeks of calm were to ease us into a false sense of security.

I steel myself and rip the envelope open. My heart stutters when photos fall to the ground. I bend to pick them up and swear out loud when I see the images. Of course, I should have known better than to play with Olivia at the market. I just wanted to make her smile and to see her light up again when her shine had dulled. The evidence of how bad an idea that was now sits right in front of me.

The photos show Olivia and me at the market. There are a couple of innocent photos of us perusing the market stalls hand in hand. But that's not what has my blood turning to ice. No, those are the photos that show Olivia with her hands placed against the crates in the alley, her dress bunched up, and my fingers inside her. The picture isn't of perfect quality, but there is no ambiguity about what we are doing there.

Like last time, there's a note, this time, it's addressed to me.

SHE'S A PRETTY LITTLE THING, ISN'T SHE? IT WOULD BE A SHAME IF SOMETHING WERE TO HAPPEN TO HER.

I can't breathe. My vision turns fuzzy around the edges, and my heart seems to be trying to beat its way out of my chest. She's in danger, and I don't know what to do. But now, I'm sure it's Darren. Olivia's photos and notes left me uncertain, but this? This is a direct threat addressed to me. Someone wants to hurt her to get to me. And there's only one person in my life twisted enough to do something like this—one person with both the motive and the audacity.

Darren. Fucking. Johns.

I stand frozen at my mailbox, photos in hand, until I'm eventually able to shake myself out of my dissociated state. Emotion floods me—rage, fear, and anxiety. I can't decide if I want to hurt someone, throw my fist through a wall, or find Olivia and whisk her away to another country where no one can find her. Or maybe all of the above.

I consider calling the police but immediately dismiss the idea. Calling them will mean having to show the photos, and then Olivia can kiss her career goodbye. I can't put her through that. This is all my fucking fault. If I'd just stayed away, none of this would be happening to her. I've been selfish. I should never have put her career at risk the way I did.

Hatred for myself and the situation courses through my veins, and without conscious thought, my fist crashes against the brick wall of the apartment building. Bone crunches and pain shoots up my hand and wrist. Blood spurts from the knuckles that made contact with the wall.

The pain is good.

The pain is grounding.

With ragged breaths, I place one foot in front of the other to walk into the apartment. Reluctantly, I grab a bag of frozen peas to put on my rapidly swelling hand. Punching the wall was another stupid mistake, but damn it felt good.

I collapse onto the sofa, forcing myself to cool the rage burning inside me so I can think clearly. I have to meet Olivia at her office soon. I didn't even want to leave in the first place, but I needed to grab a few things. At this point, I'm practically living with her.

But these photos? They're just another reminder that I need to stay by her side. I decide I won't tell Olivia about this new development. I can't forget those initial days after she received her photos, and the fear that was plastered all over her face and darkened her eyes. I don't want her to feel like that again. There's nothing we can do right now, so telling her what's going on is just going to cause her more distress.

I feel so fucking hopeless right now, but the one thing I can control is how much anxiety I allow her to suffer.

"Hey, Mom, how are you? Is everything still okay?" I ask, worry lacing my tone.

"Nate, honey, everything is the same as it was yesterday when you rang. And the day before. And the day before that," she responds with a laugh. "Darren has been out of prison for about two months now, and we haven't heard a peep. If he were going to do something to me, he would have already. He's obviously moved on and is keeping his head down. I think it's time for you to move on, too. I'm safe."

I gnaw on my lip, grateful that she's okay but suspecting that he's just changed targets. At least I don't have to split my anxiety and protection between Mom and Olivia. Days have passed since the photos I received, and Olivia is none the wiser.

"How are things with you and Olivia?" she asks. I haven't filled Mom in on the threat situation, but I have told her about Olivia. She's thrilled that I've finally found someone I can see a future with. "When can I meet her?"

"Soon, Mom," I promise. I can't wait to introduce the two most important people in my life. As mom and I chat, hands snake around my neck, and I feel Olivia's chest press against my back. Her breaths tickle my neck, and I trip over my words at the distraction.

"Mom, I've got to go. I'll call again tomorrow," I stutter out.

Mom laughs. "You don't have to call every day, honey. I promise I'm okay, and I will call you if anything happens."

"I'll call you tomorrow," I reiterate, knowing that I'll continue to check in until I'm certain that everyone I love is safe.

I end the call and turn to face my seductress, who's wearing deep red lingerie and looks like every wet dream I've ever had.

"I have an idea," she purrs, causing my dick to immediately stand to attention.

"Oh?" I ask, raising an eyebrow.

"Halloween is coming up soon," she begins, and I realize that the holiday has completely escaped my thoughts with everything going on. "I want to do something special with you," she continues. "Will you come to a party with me?"

"What kind of party?"

"The kind where the dark and depraved get to play," she replies mysteriously. "I've been keeping an eye on Hunted, and there's been talk about a Halloween party where we can all live out our darkest desires. There will be private playrooms, toys, and a safe environment where we can experiment together. There are so many things I want to try with you."

Fuck, this girl ...

She's perfect for me in every way.

"Sounds perfect," I tell her, and her lips turn up in a dazzling smile.

"Start getting your costume ready. I'm quite fond of masked men," she says with a smirk.

A mask it is then.

Olivia

I finish the final touches of my costume and makeup, and I look at myself in the mirror with satisfaction. I look spooky and hot with my face painted in a skeletal design reminiscent of the *Day of the Dead,* and my body barely covered in white lingerie—almost bridal looking. Nate's going to die when he sees me. Anticipation buzzes through my veins as I gather everything to leave.

Nate is going to meet me there. He has refused to tell me what his costume is going to be, suggesting that not knowing will enhance the excitement. He wants to hunt me again, and even with a mask on, I'm sure I'll be able to recognize him.

The building hosting tonight's party is dark and unassuming. Nothing about the outside suggests the debauchery happening within. The streets are alive with people in all sorts of costumes, ready to party the night away on one of the biggest nights of the year. New Orleans certainly does Halloween well.

I enter the building, immediately taking in the sultry mood lighting and the thumping music. I receive a wristband on entry, identifying me as someone who is in a relationship and not looking to mingle with others, and then I join the crowd of people in the club beyond.

I've never been anywhere like this before. Everywhere I look, there is another scantily dressed man or woman engaging in some form of sexual act. Moans are interspersed with the music, and bodies writhe together in varying forms of intimacy. My face heats, and I don't know where to look. I feel the need to avert my eyes, but then remember that these people are doing these things out in the open, so they must be more than happy to be seen.

In front of me, two men kiss a woman's neck; one has his hand down her skirt, and the other man kneads her breasts. Her eyes are closed and her head thrown back in ecstasy, and I can hear her moans from where I stand. My heart beats faster, and heat pools in my core. Where is Nate? I need him.

As if reading my mind, my phone vibrates with an incoming message. I tear my eyes away from the throuple I'd been watching and pull it out.

Nate

I hope you're ready to be chased, little devil.

Panties slick with arousal, my gaze wanders around the room looking for him, but I don't see anyone who looks like Nate. It's Halloween, so most people are wearing masks, but I can still make out enough of their faces and bodies to know none of them are him. I wander to the bar and order myself a shot, hoping to settle

some of my nerves about being so intimate in public. After down-
ing the shot and coughing at the burn in my throat, a prickling
sensation at my back has me turning around.

There he is.

Nate stands unmoving within the crowd, and he's covered head
to toe. Long sleeves, pants, and a full balaclava make him look far
more overdressed than anyone else here. He really did go all out
with the whole anonymity thing, didn't he?

Now that he's here, I know it's time to run. I take off through
one of the doors that opens up to a hallway lined with private
rooms. My heels click on the vinyl floors, and cries and groans echo
from beyond the doors, telling me that some of them are already
occupied.

A few doors down, I find an unoccupied room and throw open
the door. Nate still hasn't come through the door from the main
area yet, so I have time. Like the last time we played, I don't try too
hard to hide.

I want him to catch me.

And then I want him to punish me.

The room's rather luxurious compared to what I was expecting
from an establishment like this. There's a large bed in the center
of the room, and a mirror covering the ceiling. All kinds of toys
designed to inflict both pleasure and pain are lined up on a table
off to the side, and I can't help but wonder which ones Nate will
use on me when he finds me.

I position myself on the bed, posing in a way that I hope is sexy
as hell, and wait for Nate to find me. Minutes later, the sound of

the door creaking open fills the room, and then soft footfalls move to where I lie on the bed. I expect him to say something—to tell me I've been caught and will be punished, but he doesn't say anything.

I lift my head and see him standing at the end of the bed. The dim lights in the room make it almost impossible for me to make out anything other than the shape of his body. The dark clothing he's wearing also isn't helping my visibility.

"Oh no, you found me," I purr in mock surprise. "How are you going to punish me?"

He finally moves, crawling onto the bed and lowering himself down on top of me.

18

Nate

S hit! I'm running late, and I'm sure Olivia isn't going to be pleased that I've left her stranded in a sex club all alone. I was supposed to be here thirty minutes ago, but I got held up with a work emergency that couldn't wait until tomorrow. I told her I was running late, and when I was almost here, I warned her that the chase would start soon. I wonder if she's already hiding?

When I receive my wristband and enter the club, I circle the room, looking for anyone who could be her. She hasn't told me what her costume is, but I don't think she will be covered completely. I told her that I would be wearing a mask and I think I look pretty damn good in my black domino mask. I'm far from the only man here wearing one so it might take her more than a glance to notice me. I look for the telltale sign of Olivia's long blond hair, but I can't see her anywhere amongst the sexy angels, devils, vampires, and other Halloween-inspired costumes. Oh, my little devil, hiding already are we?

My first rotation of the room does not yield results, and I assume she's decided to hide away from the main crowd. Maybe she went to a private room. The thought has me thickening in my pants in anticipation.

Just to be sure I haven't missed anything, I pull out my phone and shoot her a text.

Nate

I'm here, beautiful. Where are you?

I stare at the screen, waiting for the notification that she read the message, but it doesn't come.

I'm coming, little devil.

Olivia

Heat envelops me as Nate lowers his body onto mine. He feels heavier than usual, and his body is more rigid.

"Nate, baby, is everything okay?" I ask, and again he doesn't answer.

Unease prickles my skin, and I wiggle a little to see if he will move off me. He lurches forward and grabs my wrists, positioning them above my head and using one large hand to hold them bound together. He leans into my neck and inhales deeply. I'm overwhelmed by the strong and putrid scent of stale alcohol and cigarette smoke. I gag and move my head away, confused and afraid.

Nate doesn't smoke.

What the fuck?

I squirm again, trying to release my hands as something instinctual tells me over and over that this isn't right. I don't know who this is, but I'm certain it's not Nate. That realization chills me to my core, and adrenaline floods my system.

The man's free hand roams my body, and I try to scream, but no noise escapes me. I buck my hips, and the man lets out a groan that sickens me and makes my stomach roil, but the movement does nothing to help me get away.

I need to get away.

I need to get away.

I *need* to get away.

"Naughty Olivia," rasps the man, and the words remind me of the note I received in my office. "I warned him. He took something special from me, and now I'll take something from him."

A single tear leaves a track down my cheek. "Please let me go," I whisper, my body shaking.

The man's throaty laugh echoes through the room and the sudden volume change causes me to startle. "I don't think so," he replies, and I whimper before I can stop myself.

He starts to kiss me, first on my cheek, then my neck, and over my collarbone. Terror shuts down my brain, and I can't think of a way to escape. He's so much bigger than me, and he has me pinned down.

I close my eyes and hold my breath to try and erase the vile smell and the vision of this man who wants to take from me something I'm not willing to give. Instead, I picture Nate—his warm smile and bright eyes flecked with gold, the lopsided smirk when he thinks I've said something funny, and the reverence with which he looks at me when he doesn't think I'm looking back. I picture him, to try and drown out this nightmare.

Nate

Not displaying any ounce of etiquette, I barge into private rooms looking for Olivia. The occasional scream and shout follow me, though some occupants don't even care about the interruption. Right now, I'm not interested in being a voyeur, and once I quickly ascertain that Olivia isn't here, I move on to the next room.

I quickly move through the rooms, and the longer it takes to find her, the more uneasy I become. I know this is our game, but I thought I would have found her by now. She usually makes it so easy to find her; the woman is desperate for my cock, and to be punished in whatever way I see fit. Irritation heats my skin at the fact that she's not already stark-naked underneath me right now. The chase is definitely fun, but not as fun as catching her.

I wonder if maybe she isn't in this area of the club after all. There are multiple sections of private rooms, and maybe she has gone to another. The urge to find her increases along with a twinge of anxiety that feels like someone has their fist around my heart. I try to bury the feeling and focus on the task at hand.

I search room after room with no luck and constantly check my phone to see if she's messaged me, but of course, she hasn't. Sweat pools under my mask as more and more time passes and my anxiety builds.

I return to the club's main area and start to ask around. I show a photo on my phone and ask if anyone has seen her. Most were so wrapped up in their partner or partners to pay any attention, but finally, a bartender remembers seeing her.

"Oh yeah, I remember her. Pretty skull-like makeup. I served her a shot."

"Where did she go?" I ask through gritted teeth. He gestures vaguely towards the doors leading to the rooms I've mostly already checked, and I want to scream at the lack of clear direction. Instead, I clench my fists and walk away.

Olivia

Hands grope and squeeze, each touch feeling like bugs crawling under my flesh. My eyes remain closed, and I picture myself somewhere else.

Anywhere else.

"The bastard is going to wish he never crossed me. He's finally going to get what he deserves," the man mutters erratically. He's deranged, and that fact makes my situation even more terrifying. You never know what someone as sick and twisted as this can do.

The cold bite of metal against my neck makes my eyes fly open in shock. Above me, the stranger straddles my thighs, and the glint of what I can only assume is a knife passes back and forth across my throat with only the flat part touching. I freeze, scared that any flinch or attempt to get away will have him turning the knife so that it draws blood.

The man reaches up to remove his balaclava. I don't want to see his face. Seeing his face makes everything more real, and I won't be able to pretend anymore.

I force myself not to turn away and instead, I draw upon every bit of strength I possess to stare at him, trying to show all my hatred, rage, and disgust in my eyes alone. He's removed his mask, and I'm left staring at a middle-aged man. He has dull brown hair, greying on the sides, and a slightly crooked nose—like it's been broken once or twice. His smile is twisted, like he's enjoying my fear, feeding off it.

"He couldn't just leave us alone, could he? Had to save his whore of a mother. She deserved it, she knows she did. He should never have gotten involved. He took what is mine, and now I'll take what is his." His smile is wide, and bile rises in my throat, the pieces clicking together in my mind.

This must be Darren, Nate's mother's ex-boyfriend. "Did you send me the photos?" I ask, my voice barely audible.

The laugh that escapes him is grotesque and sickening. "Sure did. And sent the ones to that bastard as well. I warned him." I stare at him in confusion, unsure of what he's referring to. My stomach sinks at the realization that Nate was hiding something from me. Did he know I was in danger and didn't tell me?

"I think I'll have some fun with you before I make him pay," he says, and my blood turns to ice. He pulls back and uses the knife to nick the side of my underwear, cutting them down the side.

When he exposes me to him, I decide that I'm not going to just lie back and take this. I'm going to fight. I don't know how, but I will.

Nate

Panic claws at my chest as I reach the last room at the end of the hallway. Of course, Olivia would go straight to the end. I shove the door open, ignoring the occupied sign. The lights are dim, but I can make out the figure of someone—likely a man, lying on top of someone on the bed.

As the door bangs shut behind me, the man shifts back to his knees and turns to face me. My stomach plummets, and my vision blackens around the edges. This has to be some kind of nightmare. It can't be real.

Darren. Fucking. Johns.

I know, without a shadow of a doubt, that the woman underneath him is Olivia.

My Olivia.

In the brief moment that my eyes meet his and a sadistic grin pulls up his lip, chaos erupts.

Olivia launches her knee straight into Darren's groin, causing him to cry out in pain.

I don't think. I just act.

Olivia

With a strength I didn't know I possessed, I use the brief moment of Darren's confusion to thrust my knee up into his crotch as hard as possible. The feel of it colliding with his—likely very small—dick is satisfying, and the scream that escapes his lips lets me know that my aim was true.

I quickly make the most of his distraction to roll out from underneath him, kicking my leg back as I do to crack him in the side. I laugh as another yelp of pain rings through the air.

"Olivia," calls a voice, and a strangled sob forces its way out of me at the recognition of Nate's voice.

He found me.

He's here to save me.

Before I get the chance to run for the door, Darren moves to face me. "You fucking bitch," he snarls and spit flies from his mouth.

Time seems to slow, and all I can hear is my heart pounding

furiously.

One heartbeat.

Someone hits me from the side with the force of a battering ram, and I fall to the floor in a heap.

Two heartbeats.

A splatter of warm liquid hits my face. At first, I'm confused, but when the coppery smell and taste reach my senses, I know what it is. Blood.

Three heartbeats.

Darren's body slumps to the floor.

Four heartbeats.

I raise my eyes to meet those of the man I'm beginning to love. There's a knife in his hand, tinged with blood. His chest rising and falling rapidly and his breaths escaping in pants. His eyes are wild and concerned as he stands frozen in place.

Five heartbeats.

Fuck.

Olivia

There's a buzzing in my ears, a hum of a thousand mosquitoes that drowns out every thought in my head. It gets louder and louder as I lie frozen on the floor. My body feels incapable of moving. I close my eyes and wonder what is causing the annoying sound.

Why is my face sticky?

My mind drifts to the clients I'm booked in to see at work on Monday. Oh, I've got that report I have to write, I almost forgot. I should probably remind myself to get started on that as soon as I get into the office.

I haven't called my parents in a while. I think I want to call them and check in. I also want to see how things are going with Tia and her girlfriend. I haven't been the best daughter or sister lately. I think I should try to change that.

"Olivia." A voice says my name, but it sounds like a whisper—an echo coming from a distant place.

I could organize a trip back to Texas to see them all. Yeah, that's a good idea. It's been far too long since I've visited.

"Olivia," calls the voice again. What does it want? I'm busy.

"Livi, you need to open your eyes for me, little devil." My eyes aren't closed. Oh, wait, they are. I don't want to open them, but I can't remember why.

My body is jostled, as if someone is shaking my shoulder. "Olivia Kane, you need to listen to me and open your eyes. We are running out of time." This time, the voice is louder, closer, and more insistent. The buzzing noise starts to recede, and I find I can't ignore the voice any longer.

I pry my eyes open and immediately want to shut them again.

Memories assault me. The metallic scent of copper—blood. The sticky substance coating me—also blood. The man who stands before me—Nate.

Oh god, what have we done?

Nate

W ide, blue eyes look up at me from the floor.

Confused.

Terrified.

We need to leave, but I can see she's going into shock, and I don't know how to snap her out of this state.

"Come on, little devil," I say quietly, trying to keep my voice soft and encouraging. "We need to get you cleaned up and out of here."

She doesn't respond. She looks at me as if she has no idea where we are or what happened. We can't wait much longer, someone will find us, and I'll be damned if we are going down for this scumbag. I was protecting Olivia, and not a single part of me regrets my choice.

I drag my eyes away from Olivia and look once more at the body of the man who attacked what is mine. I feel nothing but satisfaction as the deep crimson pool spreads beneath him. The world is a much better place without him in it.

I still have the knife in my hand; my fingers almost fused around the hilt. I drop it in disgust.

Olivia is bare from the waist down, and it takes every bit of strength I possess not to go back and stab the bastard again for good measure. I remove my button-up shirt, leaving me in just my undershirt. I tie it around her, forming a makeshift skirt. It's not perfect, but it will do.

I run through the next steps in my head, trying to determine how to get ourselves out of this mess without being caught.

Step 1. Remove fingerprints.

I hastily use the small basin in the adjoining bathroom to dampen the bottom of my shirt. I count myself lucky that Darren picked a room with a bathroom. I use my shirt to wipe every part of the knife I may have touched. Fortunately, it all happened so quickly that I touched nothing else. I place the knife down next to Darren's body, confident that all fingerprints have been removed.

Step 2. Rouse Olivia

When I return to Olivia, her vacant eyes are beginning to show some life once more.

"Nate," she whispers, and I scoop down to pick her up. She wraps her arms around my neck and buries her head into my chest. Thank god I'm wearing all black, as it masks the blood. Olivia isn't so lucky. In her white lingerie, she is looking every bit the fallen angel.

My little devil.

"Can you stand?" I ask Olivia. She nods, and I place her down.

She wobbles a little but gets her bearings and remains standing. That's my girl.

"We should turn ourselves in," she suggests in a hushed tone. "You were protecting me. He was going to—" A strangled sob prevents her from finishing that sentence, but I can fill in the blanks.

"I don't think it's a good idea. We can't prove it. No matter what, a public scandal like this could ruin your career. He wouldn't have even been here if it weren't for me. I'm going to get us out of this."

Step 3. Clean up as much of the blood as possible.

I find a washcloth and begin the process of wiping down Olivia. She is quiet again, her body unmoving. After I clean the blood off her cheeks, I pepper them with light kisses, tasting the saltiness of her tears that occasionally escape. She's trying to be strong. She *is* strong. No one should ever have to endure what she has had to tonight.

Step 4. Ensure there are no other traces of DNA.

"Livi, did you touch anything here other than the bed?" I ask gently. She shakes her head.

Good. That's good.

I take Olivia by the hand and lead her back into the room. Her gaze doesn't stray from me, and I hope that continues as I don't want her to have to see the body.

I carefully examine the bed, looking for stray hairs that may have been pulled from Olivia or rubbed off her clothes. I find a couple and place them inside the washcloth, which gets tucked into my pocket. Rage heats my blood and threatens to escape, but I shut the feeling down. There will be time to be angry later, but I need to focus on getting us out right now.

Step 5. Get the hell out of Dodge.

I hold Olivia's face in my hands, and relief floods me when I see the girl I love staring back at me. She's shaking, but I no longer see the signs of confusion and dissociation that were there before.

"We're going to leave now, okay? We will make sure the occupied sign is in place on the door and walk out like nothing has happened. We are going to act normal—like a couple that has just enjoyed the facilities and can't wait to get home to spend even more time with each other. Everyone is dressed up for Halloween, so a little bit of blood won't be that noticeable." Olivia looks down at herself and shudders.

"Can you do this, Livi?" Her nod is strong, determined. I pull her close and murmur into her hair, "I'm going to protect you."

I lead Olivia to the door and scan the room one more time, reflecting on every crime documentary I've seen and podcast I've listened to.

Have I missed anything?

This wasn't a carefully planned and executed crime, there could be evidence left behind. I just have to hope that I've done enough to remove most traces of DNA. That is likely the only way they could trace us back to Darren. We showed our IDs to get in, but that was just to prove we were of legal age. As far as I know, they haven't kept a record of who is here tonight.

I tuck Olivia under my arm, and we leave the room. As the door shuts behind us, I hope like hell that this is the last bit of stress and anguish that Darren will ever cause us again.

Olivia

The sound of ringing rouses me. It's not my cell, so it must be Nate's. I ignore it and keep my eyes firmly closed. Nate's warmth wraps around me, and I feel comfortable. Safe. That is, until I remember the events of last night, and bile rises in my throat.

Nate brought me back to his house last night and tucked me into bed. I don't remember much of what happened in between him finding me at the club and ending up here, but I think that's a good thing.

The phone stops ringing but starts again immediately. Nate groans and, with one last squeeze, releases me to roll over.

"Hey, Mom," he says, his voice weary. I can't make out the frantic words on the other end, but the urge to block my ears is strong. I can sense what's coming.

"Good. I'm glad. That fucker deserved that and more," he spits.

Another pause while his mom speaks.

"Of course I didn't. I was home with Olivia all night."

No, he wasn't.

"It's okay, Mom. You're safe now. He can't ever hurt you again. I'll see you soon, okay? I'll bring Olivia to meet you."

He ends the call and rolls back into me, pulling my back against his chest and wrapping an arm tightly around me.

"Livi, baby, are you awake?" I nod my head, and he must feel it as he moves me onto my back. I finally open my eyes and look into his, filled with concern. I can't avoid this any longer.

"Can you talk to me, little devil? Say something so I know you're okay."

"Something," I mumble, and the look of complete shock on Nate's face almost makes me laugh out loud. Almost.

"There you are," he says, placing the briefest of kisses on my lips. "Are you okay?"

Yes.

No.

Maybe.

Will I ever be okay again?

"I'm still processing," I eventually respond. That's the truth. Now that the initial shock has worn off, my emotions are conflicted. There are so many different feelings fighting against each other that I don't know what is real.

How should I be feeling?

I'm horrified and satisfied.

Disgusted and relieved.

Scared and angry.

How dare that disgrace of a human being do this to me. What gives him the right to take what doesn't belong to him? To use my body as a method of getting revenge.

Darren's words come back to me: "I warned him."

"Nate, did Darren send you a message threatening me?" I know from the stillness of his body that it's true.

"I'm sorry, Livi. I didn't know what to do. I was so stupid. Not for a moment did I think he would get to you like that." His voice shakes, and I know he's sincere, but right now, his sincerity is doing nothing to temper my rage.

"So, you just decided to keep a direct threat to my safety a secret? Chose not only not to tell me, but not even the police? Do you even care about me at all?" The words pour out of me, fueled by anger, pain, and shock.

"Livi, I—"

"No. You don't get to make decisions like this for me. You don't get to decide what's best. Especially when it puts me in danger. That's not love." I interrupt with a sob.

"But I do love you," he whispers.

That's not how our confessions of love were supposed to happen. None of this was supposed to happen.

"I need some time," I say eventually, pulling myself out of bed and away from Nate. I can't even look at him as I put on one of his t-shirts and walk out.

Nate

I'm fucking miserable.

I had everything I'd always dreamed of, and she slipped through my fingers like sand at the beach. It doesn't even seem like she's mad about the fact that I murdered a guy. What mattered most was that I lied and made decisions for her without including her. And those decisions hurt her.

She has to live with what that bastard did to her for the rest of her life, and I have to live with my actions. Is she ever going to be able to forgive me?

Even if she chooses never to come back to me, I won't ever leave her.

I've been on edge the whole week. Darren's murder has been on the news and all over social media. Every time his name is mentioned, dread pools in my gut. I don't regret what I did to him at all, but I'm afraid of going to prison. Fortunately, the police don't seem to have had any breaks in the case. It looks like I may have done enough to erase any trace of Olivia and me, but I don't want to get too complacent.

I've been following her like I used to but trying to remain inconspicuous. I don't know how she would react to it now, given the situation. Even when I was with her, there must have been some part of me that suspected things might not last between us. Or some part that didn't want to leave my stalker ways behind me. I installed cameras in her house. Small ones. Invisible ones. And I'm so grateful for that now because it allows me to keep an eye on her without being by her side.

I want to be there. I *ache* for it. But if she never forgives me, then at least I can always protect her.

I watch the live feed from her living room on my phone. She arrived home not long ago, and, after changing into her comfortable clothes, set herself up on the sofa with a blanket. I'd do anything to be the thing that makes her feel warm and safe.

It gets later into the night, but I can't draw my eyes away from her small figure on my screen. Eventually, I fall asleep and dream about her, like I do every night.

"You look like shit," Mom tells me.

"Jeez. Don't sugar coat it or anything," I reply, knowing that she's probably right. I'm not sleeping well, and the bags under my eyes are probably dark enough to show it. My dreams alternate between the good times I spent with Olivia and the horror of seeing Darren's body on top of her. Either way, I wake up exhausted, sad, and scared. I also haven't shaved in a week, and my once neat stubble is now an absolute mess.

"When was the last time you washed your clothes?" she asks, concerned. I shrug. I've got no idea. Not a great indicator. I guess I probably smell as well. What a catch I am. No wonder Olivia left me.

When Mom asked me to meet her for lunch, I was more than happy to do something other than sitting in my boxers crying about Olivia. Yeah, I know. I'm pathetic.

"What is going on with you, honey?"

"Olivia left me," I admit.

"What did you do?" she asks immediately.

"How do you know I did something?" I reply indignantly.

"I know you, Nate. Your heart is big, and you have so much love to give, but you don't always make the best decisions in your relationships."

"I made a mistake and didn't trust her with something important."

"Well, can you fix it?" she says encouragingly.

"I don't think she wants it to be fixed," I reply quietly.

"Nate James Holloway. I've never heard you talk about anyone like you talk about this woman. Do you love her?"

"More than I ever thought possible."

"Then you owe it to both of you to make this right. You won't forgive yourself if you don't try everything to get her back."

She's right. I've been respecting Olivia's need for space, but maybe I need to fight for her. I can't let her slip through my fingers. She's perfect for me.

"Tell me about her," Mom demands. And so, I do. I tell her everything I've learnt about her. I sound like a lovesick puppy, telling her how Olivia's hair shines in the sunlight, and how she snores softly but she refuses to admit it. Of course, Mom doesn't need to know any of these things, but she sits there listening with a soft smile on her face anyway.

"She sounds wonderful. I can't wait to meet her."

"Hopefully, one day you will," I respond.

"Oh, I have no doubt."

Olivia

Everything fucking sucks.

I feel like I've lost a giant part of my soul, and I've only known him for a few weeks. How is that even possible to love someone so much, so quickly?

I haven't heard from Nate since I left his apartment two weeks ago. Part of me can't help but be disappointed that he didn't chase me, and didn't try harder to stop me from leaving. He tried so hard to get me; how could he let me go so easily?

It took a day or two for the shock of what happened on Halloween to disappear fully. When it did, I realized that perhaps I was too harsh on Nate for keeping Darren's contact from me. I know he was doing what he thought he had to do to protect me. And he did protect me. When I needed him the most, he was there. He killed for me.

I'm still pissed, don't get me wrong. But the strength of that emotion definitely started to fade when the sadness of being without him began to take over.

I miss him so much.

I keep looking for him, wondering if he's still following me. Occasionally, I think I glimpse his sun-streaked hair or someone with his build, but by the time I look closer, he's gone. It must just be wishful thinking.

I've been planning a trip back to Texas to see my family. There's something about experiencing a trauma that makes you want to be close to your family again. I haven't chosen an exact date yet. If I'm being honest with myself, I'm avoiding it because I hope things will change with Nate. That maybe he will realize I'm worth fighting for.

For the past two weeks, I've been going through the motions, never really feeling present. I've been going to work and seeing my clients, despite probably not being in the right headspace to be providing anyone with therapy. It felt like taking time off would have been a giant sign above me screaming 'I was complicit in a murder'. So, I buried that shit way, way down, and pretended everything was okay. As a therapist, I know that this is one of the worst ways to deal with trauma. But we've already established that I'm making some poor choices lately. Let's just add this to the list.

I walked into the office today, barely even acknowledging Sophia. She knows something is wrong but has respected my need for space.

"Oh, Olivia. Your secret admirer has surfaced again." I stop in my tracks. Horror floods my system. My skin breaks out in a cold sweat.

"What do you mean?" I ask, my voice shaking slightly.

"You've got another delivery, you lucky thing."

He's dead. Darren's dead. He can't be sending me things. He can't be taking photos anymore

I turn around to face Sophia, terrified of what I might see. My breath escapes me in a long whoosh when I see the bouquet of blue orchids sitting in a vase on Sophia's desk. I must have completely missed them when I walked in, trying to avoid eye contact and conversation.

Nate.

My heart begins to flutter, and relief courses through my veins. Maybe he hasn't forgotten about me after all.

"There's a note here as well," Sophia tells me, handing me a sealed envelope. I take it into my office, not wanting to read it under the questioning gaze of Sophia. She's a wonderful receptionist and a good friend, but she's nosy as hell.

Livi,

These past weeks have been hell. I'm not okay without you. I need you in my life, and letting you walk away was one of the stupidest things I've ever done. I will do anything to make it up to you and make you mine again.

I love you, little devil.

Hell's not a bad place to be in as long as you're in it with me.

Nate

My eyes pool with tears, and if it weren't for the fact that my client is due to arrive in the next ten minutes, I would be desperately hunting him down to throw myself at him again. I don't even know why I was being so stubborn and holding myself back.

As the day progresses, I start to develop a plan of how to reunite with Nate. Of course, I could just go straight to him. But I want to give him something more. Something exciting.

A hunt.

At home, I start up my laptop and log into *Hunted*. I quickly search to see if *Huntern8* has posted. There's nothing since the posts I had already seen, and a feeling of relief hits me. It's not like I thought he would move on that quickly, but it's good to confirm that he hasn't sought anyone else out on this site.

I wonder how I'm going to do this. I have to ensure that he's the only one who knows where to go. I don't want a stranger accepting this hunt and surprising me. I won't ever let anything like that happen to me again. But then, what if he doesn't look at *Hunted*? He hasn't been posting, so maybe he hasn't been logging in. I ponder this for a moment before another good idea hits me. Maybe I could play a little game with him, too.

his.little.devil

> *I'm looking for someone to chase me. To hunt me, find me, punish me. But not just anyone. I'm hoping a specific person will see this. Find me in the place where we first talked about playing this game. Do you remember? I'll be waiting for you on Friday at midnight. We belong together.*

My heart's beating erratically, and there's a sense of exhilaration that I now associate with Nate. Only him.

The last thing I do before going to sleep is to send him a message.

> *Do you want to play, baby? You know where to look for the rules of the Hunt.*

I watch as the little dots move across the screen. Then stop. Then start again. And stop. In the end, it appears that Nate decides not to respond, but I'm not worried. I've given him his clues, and now we get to play the game.

Nate

I stare at the message on my phone, afraid to blink in case it disappears. It's too good to be true. But here it is, right in front of me. A message from her that offers me all my desires. This is not at all what I expected when I sent her the flowers and letter. I anticipated more radio silence. More avoidance. I was ready to work hard for her forgiveness.

Is it a trick? Is she teasing me? No. The Olivia I've come to know wouldn't do something like that. I immediately recognize the clue she has given me. The capitalization of Hunt was all I needed to lead me to *Hunted.* I scan through the posts looking for a username that could be her—I never thought to ask her about her profile. There it is. his.little.devil. The name makes me giddy with joy and relief. She's mine. And she knows it.

I read the message and my grin grows impossibly wider. *Find me in the place where we first talked about playing this game. Do you remember it?* Of course, I do. I remember every minute I spent with her.

"Have you ever followed anyone like you did me?" Olivia asks. We are walking through City Park hand in hand, and I can't wipe the smile off my face. It's been a perfect day so far, and being able to walk alongside her instead of behind her in the shadows will never cease feeling surreal.

"No. I've never wanted anyone like I want you. None of these desires existed until I saw you." The little tilt of her lips tells me that my answer pleases her.

"What are your desires?"

I consider how to answer the question. We still haven't been together long, and I know that Olivia is still trying to determine what her sexual boundaries are. Despite my eagerness to do anything and everything with her, I'm being careful to take things at her pace. We are exploring what she likes, and so far, nothing has been off limits.

"I want to hunt you," I admit. She turns her blue eyes to me in curiosity.

"What would that look like?"

"We would find a place with no one around. You would run from me, and after a head start, I'll chase you. If I catch you, I get to do what I want with you. But you will always have the power to use your safe word. Everything will end the moment you use it. No matter what, you are always in control."

Her teeth tug on her luscious lower lip while she mulls over my words. Her cheeks have turned a soft pink, and her chest is rising with her quickened breaths. She's turned on by the idea. I know it.

"What do you think?" I ask.

"I think ... I can't wait to play." My pulse spikes, and I hold myself back from throwing her to the ground. It's possible that I might be able to have everything I've ever dreamed of.

The thought of her coming back to me makes all my worries from the last two weeks disappear.

For the first time since she left me, my hand ventures down my pants to grip my rapidly hardening cock. *We belong together.* That's what she said. She wants me, and she wants to be hunted.

I touch myself with long, languid strokes as I picture myself chasing her through the park with the only light coming from the moon. I hear her squeal of surprise when I inevitably find her and push her down into the dirt.

I groan as I thrust into my hand, imagining that it is her warm cunt that embraces me and clenches tight around me. Groans escape me as my hips move faster and I barrel towards my release. I close my eyes and try to forget that I'm alone right now. Friday is too far away. How can I possibly survive the next few days when I know what awaits me?

I spill into my hand with a cry as the image of Olivia submitting fills my mind. I want her to fight me off initially. To push me and try to roll away, all the time knowing that she will eventually submit. I want her trust and faith that I won't hurt her, and while the struggle may turn me on, I would never do anything to hurt her.

I want *everything.*

Olivia

11:30 p.m.

The clock seems to be moving forward at an impossibly slow speed. I'm already at the park. I couldn't keep pacing around my apartment in anticipation; I'd wear a hole in the carpet. I can't stop the jittery feeling lighting up my nerves.

Over the past few hours, each emotion has been warring for dominance, with a new one taking the lead every few minutes.

Excitement. What will it feel like to be chased?

Nervousness. What if he doesn't come?

Fear. What if allowing him back into my life is the wrong thing to do?

Desire. I need him.

I'm driving myself crazy.

I find somewhere to sit and mindlessly scroll through my phone while really just watching the clock tick over every minute. I'm listening out for any sound of him, adrenaline flooding my veins as midnight gets closer and closer.

12:00 a.m.

My phone beeps with a notification.

Nate

Time to run, little devil.

Without wasting a second in doubt, I bolt into the trees, a giggle breaking free before I force myself to be silent. The only sounds are the snapping of branches and my gasping breaths. There's no sign of him so far, but I know he's here.

After a few minutes of running, I stop to catch my breath. I wait, hidden in the darkness, my heart pounding against my ribs and my skin pebbling in the cool night air.

"Oliviaaaa," comes a taunting voice from my left.

I run, and this time, heavy footsteps sound behind me. Twigs get caught in my hair as I run through trees, and I make every effort to avoid rolling my ankle on any of the trip hazards underfoot. I've abandoned any hope of being silent now. He's on me, and I know he won't give up. There's no way I can outrun him.

I duck behind a large rock and wait.

A hand grabs my ankle, and I'm dragged out from my hiding spot. "Got you, little devil."

I scream, and Nate laughs. If I didn't know that I was safe with him, his laughter would concern me, but I remember our talk last time we were here. He said I am in control. One mention of my safe word, *pineapple,* and everything stops.

I kick out with my other foot and manage to get him in the

stomach. He grunts and loosens his grip on my ankle. Without delay, I jump up and try to get away. In moments, I feel the impact of his body against mine as he pushes me to the ground, quickly rolling me over so that I'm facing him.

There's a trickle of unease that runs through me at the feel of being held down. A reminder of Darren, I'm sure, but I refuse to let Darren take up any more space in my head. I will not let him taint my relationship with Nate, or have any impact on the way I choose to be with him. He's already done too much. I know that there might be some level of anxiety that stays with me, that's to be expected after a experiencing a traumatic event, but I will work through it. I'm not alone.

I focus on the feeling of Nate's body and the glimpse of him I can see in the moonlight.

It's Nate. *My* Nate. I know that I'm safe.

He holds me, pinned by my wrists, and the dirt scratches the bare skin not covered by my activewear. I wasn't really sure what one is supposed to wear when they are being chased through a park, sexually and consensually. Activewear seemed like my best option, albeit not very sexy.

I struggle half-heartedly in his grip, but I know that he's got me.

"Submit," Nate demands.

"No," I growl and continue to thrash beneath him.

He buries his head into my neck, and this time the words are softer. "Submit."

His mouth moves over my neck and to my mouth. I find myself pushing my hips up into him, desperate for friction. My breaths come in short gasps, and I let out a squeal of shock when he forcefully pulls my shorts down, leaving me bare before him.

"Fuck, I've missed you so much," he whispers, as he looks down at me from his knees. "I can't be gentle with you tonight."

"Then don't be," I reply confidently, not a flicker of doubt in my soul.

He reaches down and unzips the front zip of my sports bra. I planned ahead for easy access. My breasts spill out and Nate groans at the sight, pulling out his cock and giving it a few quick strokes.

"Are you done running?" he asks me, and the intensity in his eyes tells me he's not just talking about tonight.

"I'm not going to run anymore," I reply honestly.

"Thank fuck," he moans as his lips capture mine. His hands grip mine above my head, in a position of restraint that I now know he loves. I feel the entire length of his body pressing me into the earth. I'm only slightly aware of the small rocks and branches digging into my back, but I'm more than happy to ignore that when the feeling of Nate against me is so exquisite.

Our mouths move together in a bruising kiss. We've only been apart for two weeks, but I don't ever want to be away from him again. My body arches up into his, desperate for more than kisses. He takes my cue, reaching down and positioning himself at my entrance.

Without hesitation, he enters me, and the night air is filled with the sound of our cries. He rocks back onto his knees and draws mine up to my chest. The position allows him to move impossibly deeper, and to my surprise, my climax builds quicker than ever before.

He positions his hands on my inner thighs, spreading them wider for him, as he thrusts hard and fast without mercy. I can barely move, barely think. This is like nothing I've ever experienced.

My orgasm crashes over me, and I scream, but Nate's not finished with me yet. He doesn't yield for a second, instead increasing his pace so that my first release is barely over before the next one starts to build.

"You. Are. Mine," he grunts with every thrust.

"I'm yours," I pant. "I'm yours. I'm yours. I'm yours."

Sweat slicks our skin, and the tension in Nate's body warns me that he's close.

"I love you," I tell him, and with a roar, he spills himself inside me. The feeling of him swelling and pulsing is enough to push me over the edge for the second time, and my cry joins his.

He collapses on top of me as we gasp for air. With our foreheads pressed together, eyes closed in bliss, I give him my truth one more time. "I love you, Nate."

"God, Livi, I've loved you for longer than I've known you. You are everything to me."

We lie in silence for a few more moments, neither of us wanting to move.

"We are going to have to do this again," I tell him, and I feel his chuckle all the way through my body.

"Hell yeah, we are."

Nate

3 Months Later

Slap. The sound of the crop on her bare ass has her screaming and crying out my name. Her pussy clenches around me, and I try desperately not to fall over the edge.

"More," she pants, and of course, I oblige.

Slap. Slap. Slap. Three more hits ring out as I alternate between cheeks, relishing the pink that flushes her skin.

Every moment that I'm not buried within Olivia Kane is a moment wasted. Fortunately, I think she feels the same, if her insatiable sex drive is anything to go by.

After reuniting in the park that night, we returned to her apartment and had the conversation we should have had the morning after Darren's murder. I apologized profusely for keeping things from her—even got on my knees to beg for her forgiveness, but it was unnecessary; she'd already forgiven me. She told me that she recognized that her reaction was mostly shock from what had happened that night, and that after she had calmed down, she could think more rationally.

She made me promise never to keep anything like that from her again, which I did enthusiastically.

I told Olivia about the cameras in her apartment to keep my word. Kind of expecting her to be upset by the revelation, I was surprised when all she did was laugh.

"You knew?" I asked, perplexed.

"Well, not for certain, but I did think it was a definite possibility. You are a stalker after all."

Fair point.

I roll Olivia over onto her back, barely pulling out before thrusting into her again. Her wide, blue eyes gaze up at me with dilated pupils, and she pulls my lip into her teeth, biting down hard. I drag the riding crop across her bare stomach, pausing my movements briefly and causing a whine to escape her. Knowing that I have her exactly where I want her, I purposely tease her by patting her clit softly with the crop.

"I swear to god, Nate. If you don't make me come in the next thirty seconds, I won't let you see my tits for a week."

Fuck, she has me there.

I pound into her over and over, giving her exactly what she wants, and just when she's crying out that she's going to come, I slap her clit with the crop, and she detonates.

As we are both coming down from another mind-blowing orgasm—I swear, I'll never get sick of this—I roll over to check the time on my phone. I wasn't expecting Olivia to jump me when I walked through the door this afternoon, but I shouldn't have been surprised.

"Is your mom still coming over for dinner?" Olivia asks, and I nod in answer.

Well, that's what she thinks is going to be happening, anyway.

"I guess I'd better go shower," she tells me, untangling her limbs from mine.

Excitement bubbles away under my skin, but I try my best not to let it show. Mom's not coming over for dinner. But she is bringing over a surprise. One that I've been planning since the moment Olivia agreed to move into my apartment with me two months ago.

Just as I suspected, Mom and Olivia get along amazingly, and when I told her what I had planned, she wanted to be involved.

When she emerges from the bathroom, her hair falling around her face beautifully, I have to remind myself that my mom is going to be here any moment, so I can't fuck her again. I'm not too disappointed, though, when I think about how she is going to react to my surprise.

There's a knock on the door, and I call out to Olivia to ask if she can answer it. I follow her and watch as she warmly greets Mom.

"What's this?" she asks, reaching to take the heavy box out of Mom's hands.

"Oh, just a gift from Nate that I wanted to bring over," Mom replies with a smirk.

"Ah, exciting," Olivia exclaims, moving away from the door so that Mom can enter.

She places the large box down on the floor and looks at the holes in the lid with confusion.

"What is this?" she asks again.

"Open it," I tell her, unable to keep the smile off my face any longer.

She lifts the lid, and the squeal that escapes her is at a decibel I'm quite certain humans should not be able to produce. She reaches into the box and gently lifts out the pug puppy I bought for her. I'd picked her out myself after searching for a reputable breeder for the past few months. Even though I'd already met the adorable thing, I melt all over again when I see her tentatively lick Olivia's face, and Olivia bursts into tears.

"You got me a pug?" she sobs.

"Of course I did. I know everything about you, remember? I know you couldn't have one in your apartment, but I don't have those rules."

"We get to keep her?" she asks timidly, as if afraid I'm going to reach over and pull her out of her hands.

"We get to keep her," I confirm, and the smile that lights up her face is one I'm always going to remember.

"She doesn't have a name yet. Would you like to give her one?"

She stares at the puppy for a few moments in deep concentration.

"Bug," she says eventually.

"Huh," I ask, confused.

"That's her name. Bug the pug."

"We can't call her Bug," I say in mock horror.

"Yes, we can, and we are. Aren't we, little Buggy Boo?" she coos, smooshing her face into the puppy's fur.

"I guess we have a pug named Bug."

Acknowledgements

My biggest thanks for this book goes to my wonderful beta readers- Caity, Ash, Sarah, KJ, Alysia, Brooke, and Crystal. You have all been amazing supporters of my writing and this novella.

Thank you to my street team and anyone who has read my writing. It means the world to me to have people reading and enjoying my stories, and without my street team to spread the word, I wouldn't be able to keep doing this.

Of course, my editor Dany and my proofreader Erin deserve a massive thanks for ensuring Limerence is at it's best to share with the world.

Finally, I owe everything to my husband and children who have been the biggest practical and emotional support for this writing venture. My husband is the reason that writing cinnamon roll MMC's comes so naturally to me!

About the author

Bec Eden is an indie romance author who can always be found with a book in her hand. She loves romance books of all types and writes a range of different sub-genres. One thing you can guarantee, is that her writing will always have swoon-worthy characters and high heat.

Bec lives in Adelaide, South Australia with her husband and two very sweet and energetic boys. She loves to travel and has always been an adrenaline junkie (although the older she gets, the less this is the case!). Mostly, she prefers to be a homebody, curled up on the couch with a good book and her caramel scented candles.

Stay up to date on new announcements
Instagram and Facebook: @bookishspiceandeverythingnice
TikTok: @bec_eden_author
Website: becedenauthor.com

Also by Bec Eden

A Song of Death and Desire
A spicy little mermaid retelling.
Available now.